MW01034243

BABY BOMBSHELL

———

LAUREN CANAN

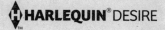

H HARLEQUIN® DESIRE

Recycling programs
for this product may
not exist in your area.

ISBN-13: 978-0-373-73399-6

Lone Star Baby Bombshell

Copyright © 2015 by Sarah Cannon

Printed in U.S.A.

Lauren Canan, born and raised amid the cattle ranches of Texas, climbed a fence and jumped onto the back of her first horse at age three. She still maintains the punishment was worth the experience. She grew up listening to her dad tell stories of make-believe and was always encouraged to let her imagination soar. The multi-award-winning author and recipient of the 2014 Golden Heart® Award happily spends her days penning her favorite kind of stories: those of two people who, against all odds, meet, fall in love and live happily ever after—which is the way it should be. In her spare time she enjoys playing guitar, piano and dulcimer in acoustic club jams and getting lots of kisses and wags from her four-legged fuzzy babies. Visit Lauren's website at laurencanan.com. She would love to hear from you!

Books by Lauren Canan

HARLEQUIN DESIRE

Terms of a Texas Marriage
Lone Star Baby Bombshell

Special thanks to two brilliant authors
who kindly gave their time and expertise.
Kathleen Gregory, I could not have done this without you.
Angi Morgan, you are my forever hero!
Thank you for all you do.

To Jill Marsal of the Marsal-Lyon Literary Agency.
You made all the difference.
Thank you for believing in me.

To my editor, Charles Griemsman,
for your endless patience and encouragement.
You are the best.

To Laurel Hamrick for being there
when I needed to whine!

And to Terry, my real-life hero, who taught me
the true meaning of love and happily-ever-afters.

One

Kelly Michaels slowed the car as she neared the twelve-foot-high black wrought-iron gates banked by native stone walls on either side. A bronze plaque on the left welcomed her to the C Bar Ranch. She stretched to reach the keypad and entered the code Don Honeycutt, the Realtor, had provided.

With a resounding *click*, the gates swung open, separating the giant *C* set in the center. She followed the long winding drive flanked by centuries-old oak trees towering over lush green pastures. She pulled around to the staff entrance. The home was enormous. It was more mansion than typical ranch house. But new construction was generally a breeze to clean. Gathering the implements out of the trunk, she went inside.

Her instructions were to clean two bedrooms and adjoining baths upstairs plus the den, office, foyer and kitchen downstairs. She should be able to wrap this up in time to get ready for the annual music festival and dance that evening. The generous pay she earned occasionally cleaning new homes for the local Realtor was more than worth the effort. It had once been her only income, but even after she landed a job consistent with her field of study, she'd held on to this one and the financial bonus it offered.

She started on the second-floor master suite, working her way downstairs. Some furniture had been delivered. New bedding and pillows lay on the mattresses. Kelly quickly and efficiently put everything in order. An interior designer would probably complete the rooms in accordance with the new owner's preferences.

She loved the smell and freshness of a new home. Holidays in this house would be amazing. A turkey roasting in the oven while pumpkin and coconut pies cooled on the dark granite counters. The aroma of spices and home-baked bread filling the air. She could imagine laughter and teasing banter filling the great space while children played hide-and-seek around a huge tree. She envied the family who would live here. At least, she hoped it was a family. The gossip around town said the old ranch had been purchased by an out-of-state corporation for employee retreats. It would be a shame if no one actually lived in this beautiful home.

A couple hours later, while rinsing the last of the soap from the kitchen sink, she heard the door in the utility room open and close. Must be Don checking on her progress. She smiled, knowing she'd completed the house, just as requested.

"Kelly?"

The breath caught in her throat and all outward motion stopped. The voice did not belong to Don Honeycutt. Her heart slammed against the walls of her chest as denial overwhelmed her mind. *It couldn't be.* Bracing herself against the counter, she turned and stared incredulously at the man standing less than four feet away.

"Jace." His name came out a whisper, a testament to the pure shock pummeling her from every direction. She blinked her eyes, willing her mind to convey it was only an illusion.

But the illusion was very real.

In the year since she'd seen him, he'd changed very little. His rugged good looks hadn't diminished. If anything, he appeared even more handsome than before, something she wouldn't have thought possible. The deep line of his jaw was smooth now, missing the bearded shadow he'd had before. His dark hair was cut several inches shorter. The tiny scar was still visible, the only imperfection of full lips that could widen into a devilish grin showing perfect white teeth, a smile irresistible to most everyone, male or female, young or old.

Kelly swallowed hard. She knew the touch of those lips. A man in his prime, he took extraordinary care to stay in top physical condition. It was, after all, part of his job. Part of who he was. She hadn't known it before, but she certainly knew it now.

"What are you doing here?" His deep, graveled voice mirrored her surprise, sending goose bumps over her skin.

With a wet sponge in one hand and a can of powdered cleanser in the other, she thought the answer should be obvious.

"I might ask you the same question." But she feared she already knew the answer. The giant *C* on the front gate apparently stood for Compton. Suddenly the huge mansion took on the dimensions of a shoe box as the walls came crashing in. "You bought this ranch?" She needed to hear him confirm her worst fears.

"Yeah. I did."

Her heart dropped to her knees. "I...I've just finished. I'll get out of your way."

She grabbed the mop, broom and bucket of cleaning paraphernalia and without another glance in his direction, headed for the door, her mind spinning.

"Kelly, wait. You don't have to—"

She ignored him and all but ran through the side door. Why would Jace Compton, a man with the world at his fingertips, move to this tiny Texas town?

The outside lamp over the side porch provided dim light against the growing darkness. She tossed the cleaning supplies inside the car, not caring where they landed. Her hands shook so severely it took three tries to insert the key into the ignition of the twenty-year-old Buick. It responded in kind, quivering equally as badly as her hands while the engine struggled to engage. After she'd made several attempts and repeated silent pleas to *start*, it became clear the old car wasn't going anywhere.

This couldn't be happening.

Her cell phone lay on the seat next to her, but even if it found a signal there was no one to call. By now her friends were at the music festival along with most of the county. It was the single largest event of the year in their small community, and she would not spoil their evening even though it was a long walk home. If only Mrs. Jenkins, her babysitter, could still drive. She had a nagging fear in the pit of her stomach that this downward spiral had not yet reached rock bottom.

Resting her forehead against the steering wheel, she closed her eyes, giving in to the memories flooding her mind, to the sharp pain once again slicing her heart into tiny pieces. The best and the worst wrapped up in one package. And the name on the label was Jace Compton.

When she'd first tried to reach him at the cell number he'd provided, she got at a voice mail message that Jace Compton—not Jack Campbell, the name he'd given her when they met—was out of the country. And the mailbox was full. Who was Jace Compton? A call out to the ranch where he'd claimed he worked provided the answer. The man to whom she'd given her heart, body and soul, the man who'd said she was so special he never wanted to let her go, was not Jack Campbell, the ranch hand. He was Jace Compton, an award-winning actor and multi-millionaire living in California, having some fun at her expense. The ranch foreman had given her another number to try, but it was disconnected.

As the memories of that day surfaced once again, shame rolled over her in a mind-numbing wave just as it had for months after she'd learned the truth. She'd been so stupid. Her initial awareness that he looked familiar had been easily dismissed with a "Yeah. I get that a lot." No doubt he would have had a pat answer even if she'd asked more point-edly. He'd set out to seduce her and she'd fallen hard. She'd wanted to believe him, to trust him, so any suspicions that he might not be who he claimed were ignored.

Weeks after he'd left, when she finally learned his true identity, it seemed as if his picture was everywhere. Photos and headlines depicting the wild beach parties, shocking affairs with married women and his playboy lifestyle in general headlined the rag sheets at the grocery store checkout lines and the celebrity programs on television.

She'd finally managed to track down his manager, who had been clear and threatening. She meant nothing to Mr. Compton. They'd had a fling. So what? Jace had lots of flings. Unless she was prepared for a court battle over custodial rights, which Jace would assuredly win, she should take the manager's advice and handle the situation herself. Numbly, Kelly had hung up the phone. She hadn't slept that night. Or the next. She'd just sat in the little wooden chair in her bedroom and stared at nothing while her mind bounced between disbelief and utter devastation.

Nine months later, as she lay in the hospital bed praying for her baby to survive the complications of the birth, one of the hospital volunteers brought Kelly a magazine to read. On the front cover, the charismatic, drop-dead gorgeous Jace Compton had again been named Bachelor of the Year. The handsome face seemed to mock her as the tears spilled over and ran down her face.

Why had he come back?

After a year she thought she'd finally put it all behind her. The tears and sleepless nights, the regrets and countless waves of humiliation as time after time her mind relived how easily she'd fallen for his deception. Yet at the same time, despite the lies, the yearning for his touch refused to go away. The memories of his incredible smile fading to a look of serious intent; the knowing glint in his eyes seconds before his lips covered hers, taking her fully, deeply, until she never wanted him to let her go. His powerful arms holding her, his hard body locked to hers, his hot breath and deep voice teasing, whispering sinful things in her ear, tempting her in ways she'd never imagined, always leaving her gloriously satisfied yet wanting more.

Apparently, he hadn't had the same sentiments. If those thoughts ever entered his head, he'd quickly pushed them away. From the minute he'd boarded the plane back to California, she'd become a distant memory. To him it had just been a vacation in the north Texas ranching community with her supplying a few fringe benefits on the side.

Two raps on the car window brought her back to the here and now. Determined to keep her anger at bay, she pushed open the door and Jace took a step back. Standing at a height of well over six feet, he was wearing well-worn jeans that hugged long, muscular legs. His left arm rested on the door frame while his right settled on the roof, effectively trapping her within the boundary of his heavy arms. Getting out of the car brought her within mere inches of the hard wall of his chest. Muscles rippled under the ash-gray T-shirt, the sleeves stretching to accommodate thick biceps.

Kelly didn't want to be this close to him. She didn't want to look into his eyes, but his large stature blocked everything else as if he was purposely giving her no choice. Finally, she looked up, their gazes locked, and for an instant, time stopped. It was still there. In the deep green depths a flicker of the raw passion that once bound them together with such intensity, a passion that slam-dunked any rational thought into nonexistence.

The scent of expensive cologne surrounded her. In spite of the months of heartache, some small part of her still yearned for his touch, which was nothing short of insanity. What she needed was for him to disappear. Again.

"Please step back and let me pass." Her voice, raw with unreleased emotion, held fierce determination. He did as she asked and dropped his arms to his side. "I'll have the car off your property as soon as possible."

Without a backward glance, Kelly took off down the driveway on foot.

"Don't you have a phone? Someone you can call?"

She ignored him and increased her pace.

"You want to use mine?" She heard him mutter a curse.

Her complete focus was to get off this property and away from him as fast as possible. Her mind was still reeling from the fact that he was here. He'd bought land and built a large house, usually an indication of permanency. The thought did nothing to brighten her spirits. Somehow she should have prepared for this even though logic was screaming *how could you have known*? But he had friends in the area. He'd been staying with them when they first met. He'd commented many times that he loved the general region. Why had she never considered the possibility that he would come back? She was an idiot. And now she was going to pay for it.

She didn't hear the truck on the concrete driveway until Jace pulled up next to her.

"Kelly, you can't walk all the way to town. It has to be close to six or seven miles and it's almost dark."

Hearing him so close once again still had the same effect. Her body came to life as irrational hunger for him ran rampant. She clenched her teeth and pulled the evening air deep into her lungs as tears of resentment burned her eyes. She refused to let them fall. He was right about it getting dark. And he'd guessed right about the distance. But she kept walking. She'd be every kind of fool to climb inside that truck.

In spite of her refusal to stop, he continued to roll along next to her.

"Kelly, get in the truck and let me take you home."

"No. Thank you."

The tall gates opened as she reached the end of his property. She went through them and cut to the left onto the white-rock county road. The gravel made it harder to walk, but she refused to slow her pace. The Bar H Ranch was just a couple of miles away. Shea, her husband, Alec, or one of their ranch hands would give her a ride home. In hindsight, she should have called, but her only thought was to get away from Jace. Surely everyone hadn't gone to the festival. But if they had, she would sit on the porch and wait.

Why did Jace have to come back to Calico Springs? It was a small community where everybody knew one another. Eventually someone would tell him about Kelly Michaels and the baby who almost died when he was born four months ago. And Jace would know. He would do the math and figure out the baby was his. Another wave of panic slammed into her. What was she going to do? What *could* she do?

The iron gates clanged shut and she realized he was no longer following her. Apparently, he'd only driven to the end of his driveway and turned back. Good enough. The farther away he stayed the better. Taking a deep breath, she willed her heart to slow its pace.

The consequences of Jace finding out about Henry were beyond comprehension. She had to steel herself against the urge to break into a dead run to more quickly get home to her baby. Regardless of how much money he had and how well he could lie, Jace was not getting custody, no matter what she had to do or where she had to go.

The sun had set, darkening the sky to deep purple. Shadows of the trees and tall grass along the road faded into the overall darkness of the landscape. She wished for a flashlight. Even though the road was still easy to distinguish from the surroundings, the creatures that might slither out to soak up the last of the afternoon warmth were not.

The thought brought her to a heightened sense of awareness. A wrong step might land her in a world of trouble and there was no one in shouting distance if she needed help. If anything happened to her, who would care for Henry?

Right now, her baby should be enjoying his bath before going to sleep thanks to the wonderful woman who kept him while Kelly worked. Because of the festival, no one expected her home early. She swallowed back the touch of alarm. *Think positive.* Once she reached the Bar H Ranch she'd be home free.

As if to dispute that optimistic thought, lightning flashed across the sky followed by deep, rolling thunder. Kelly groaned, not daring to think this night could get any worse.

Jace Compton took in a deep breath of frustration, his jaw muscles working overtime. He couldn't believe Kelly had been in his house. Cleaning it, no less. How bizarre was that? He'd hoped he could find her if he moved to Calico Springs. But he never considered she'd be in the house, and he wasn't prepared for the immediate anger and the glaring gaze shooting beams of blue-green fire in his direction.

Apparently, she'd found out he'd lied about his identity when he was here before. He hoped she would give him a chance to explain. He'd had twenty-five precious days on a neighboring ranch to kick back, relax and be himself, just a guy who'd grown up on the south side of Chicago. The last thing he wanted was someone to discover his identity. Over the years he'd become proficient at staying well under the radar. He'd had no idea when they first met that their relationship would develop into something so much more.

Kelly had accepted that he was a cowhand from a nearby ranch, and there had never been a right time to tell her differently. In hindsight he hadn't wanted to take a chance on putting a wedge between them and that special something they'd found in each other. It was a timeless journey where they were the only two people in the world. It was perfect. When she returned his kisses, he'd known she was kissing *him*, the regular guy, not the wealthy celebrity. It was a damn good feeling. When the time came to leave, he wrestled with his conscience, wanting to tell Kelly the

truth. Finally he decided to wait until he returned to Calico
Springs. He hadn't expected the four-month interim period
he'd planned to expand to over a year.

On the outside, the Kelly he remembered had changed,
and those changes immediately had his libido sitting up
and taking notice. The curves of her body were decidedly
more feminine, more mature, more alluring than those of
the model-thin young woman he remembered. She exuded
health and considerably more sex appeal than he recalled,
making him wonder how he'd ever torn himself away. The
long blond locks that used to flow free and silky around
the delicate features of her face were pulled to the back of
her head in a ponytail, giving her face a different, intensely
alluring quality, accenting the almond shape of her eyes.
Jace had never seen eyes that color. They were the same
brilliance and shade as the turquoise waters of the Medi-
terranean. Only tonight, instead of containing a welcoming sparkle, they'd reflected more than a small trace of
annoyance when she stared at him as if the devil himself
had come to life.

While he'd anticipated she would be a bit perturbed if
she learned he'd lied about his identity, he didn't expect the
high level of animosity she'd shown today. Was she angry
because he'd lied or was it because she'd missed an opportunity to gain some of the wealth? Thinking of Kelly in that
light didn't sit well. At all.

Some people thought they'd found the proverbial pot of
gold when they caught his attention, a fact that galled Jace
to his core. People always wanted something, whether it was
money or five minutes worth of fame. Making action films
was his job. Not who he was. He hated the phony facade he
had to maintain, and the ridiculously implausible stories he
had to validate all for the sake of keeping his name in the
media, all to keep the publicity going. Finding someone who
liked him for himself was a rarity. He hoped Kelly would
understand. He really hoped she would.

When he'd returned to California, he'd talked nonstop about the young woman he met in Texas. He'd even mentioned buying a place to be close to her until she finished her degree. Two days later, his manager, Bret, handed him a PI report indicating Kelly was a con artist with a rap sheet a mile long, citing numerous jailed offenses. Jace hadn't wanted to believe it then and still had a hard time believing it now.

By the time six months had passed, with the filming of his latest movie hitting one roadblock after another, it no longer mattered if she had a record or not. He probably would never see her again. He'd felt more than a small twinge of loss at the thought. He'd managed to push their time together to the back of his mind until Garret Walker, the friend who had invited him to Texas, called asking if he was still interested in buying some land in the area. Suddenly in his mind's eye, all he saw was Kelly. The memories of holding her in his arms and the pure enjoyment he'd found being with her far outweighed any past crimes she may have committed. He kept Bret's warning in mind. He'd be a fool not to. But Kelly Michaels just didn't fit the mold of a crook. Perhaps she'd had a rough life? They'd never spoken in detail about her past, so all he could do was speculate. But after the way she'd almost run from his house today, it probably didn't matter one way or the other. Apparently she'd made her decision that their relationship would not continue. While he couldn't justify it in his mind, he once again felt a deep loss.

He rubbed the back of his neck. Kelly was out there in the dark, determined to walk all the way to town. He'd returned to the house to give her a chance to calm down and allow him time to get a grip. The instant he'd recognized her, his body had surged to readiness while a vapor of heat surrounded him. It was the same reaction he'd felt the very first time he'd ever seen her in the local feed store when he'd gone with Garret to place an order. The immediate attraction had overwhelmed him then, and today was no different. It was like a giant magnet pulling them together regardless of the circumstances. And when she'd stepped out of her car and her incredible scent of spring rain and nutmeg reached him, he hadn't wanted to move away, his body immediately swelling with need.

But with Kelly, it went beyond physical beauty and sex appeal, although she had plenty of that to turn any man's head. It was the look in her eyes that made him believe he could accomplish anything. Hell, when he'd held her in his arms he could fly. Her soft Southern drawl and impish nature had him bouncing off the walls and loving every second. Had it all been an act? He still didn't know the answer and probably—sadly—never would.

Raindrops began to splatter against the windowpane. He turned toward the door, intent on giving her a ride into town. His glance fell on the thin strap of a pale pink purse hanging over the back of a kitchen chair. As he lifted it from the chair back, the sound of thunder rolled over the house, followed by flashes of lightning.

With purse in hand, he headed back to the truck, ignoring the first heavy raindrops. Whether she was angry with him or not, he wasn't about to leave her outside in the dark and the quickly approaching storm. He'd make sure she got home safely, this time accepting no excuses.

Whether she liked it or not.

Two

Isn't this gonna be a basket full of fun?

Kelly eyed the sky as the thunder rumbled overhead. She didn't dare tempt fate by asking what else might go wrong. Picking up the pace, she topped the next hill just as a bolt of lightning struck a tree straight ahead. Seconds later, the sky opened up and a downpour provided the answer to her unspoken question.

Crossing her arms over her chest, she gritted her teeth and kept walking. The warm temperatures of the afternoon took a nosedive as the chilling rain continued to hammer away, stinging her face, making it hard to see. The strong wind gusts made each step forward a challenge to her determination.

Suddenly the glare of headlights from behind illuminated the road and the white blanket of rain ahead of her. She moved to the right, hoping it wasn't a bunch of liquored-up high school kids out for an evening of fun and harassment. She got her wish, but not in a way she'd wanted.

"Kelly," Jace's voice barked through the darkness as he pulled up beside her. "Get in the truck."

She continued walking.

"You're being a complete idiot," he insisted.

"You're entitled to your opinion." She had to yell to be heard over the downpour.

"You have ten seconds to get your ass inside this truck."

"Or what?"

"Or I'm going to pick you up and put you in here myself."

She turned to face him, her eyes narrowing in a glare.

"Get. In. Now." The darkness concealed his expression, but his angry tone came across loud and clear. She had little doubt he'd do exactly what he threatened.

Just do it and get home to Henry.

She looked from Jace to the dark, seemingly endless road ahead. A blustery gust of rain-filled wind assisted the return of her sanity. Biting her tongue, she walked to the truck and opened the passenger door.

"I'm wet," she unnecessarily disclosed, taking in the truck's beautiful interior.

He muttered a curse. "Everything is wet. I don't care. Get in the damn truck." His demand was accented by a loud crack of lightning directly overhead. She grabbed the hold-bar above the opening and pulled herself up and inside, closing the door behind her. Jace immediately raised the passenger window.

In the warmth of the cab, her teeth began to chatter as uncontrolled shivers assailed her body. Jace quickly adjusted the heat. The new-car smell and the earthy scent of his cologne swirled in the warm air around her. She leaned back against the rich leather and buckled her seat belt. Without another word, Jace hit the gas, sending the truck speeding toward town.

Town. Home. Kelly didn't want him to know where she lived. It took away the small sense of protection, even if it was only an illusion. In Calico Springs, population six thousand, it wasn't hard to find anybody.

"Just take me to the ranch up ahead. The entrance is on the left. I know the owners. They'll drive me the rest of the way home."

No response.

As the big truck ate up the miles, she anxiously searched to the left of the headlights for the big gate to the Bar H Ranch. Finally, the reflection of the stone pillars shone just ahead.

"There," she pointed. "Just pull in..."

The truck didn't slow as it approached, then passed, the driveway.

"You missed it." She looked behind them. "Turn around."

Jace glanced at her, then returned his focus to the road. "No reason to force anyone else out in this weather."

"*Force* anyone else? Like I forced you to be out here?" she challenged, still resenting the fact that he'd coerced her inside the truck to begin with. Never mind that she was grateful to be out of the storm.

"That's not the way I meant it. Of course you didn't." He glanced over as she sat back in the seat, her arms crossed over her chest. "And you didn't leave your handbag in my kitchen on purpose." He held up the small rectangular purse. "And you didn't know it was my house you were cleaning or that I would be arriving around six. Kelly, if you want to see me again...just say so."

Kelly's head snapped around, her jaw dropping. "Stop this truck."

Instead of slowing, he asked, "Shall I take that as a no?" as a grin spread over his handsome features.

"Yes."

"Yes?"

"Yes, I mean no."

Jace pursed his lips as though holding back another grin. "Your sense of humor isn't quite as good as I remember."

"No? Try saying something remotely funny."

He made no further comment. Kelly glared at him for another few seconds before she sat back in the seat, expelled an angry breath and accepted her fate. It was surreal. To not see him for so long, then to suddenly be in the close confines of a pickup cab as they barreled into the darkness. She glanced at him from the corner of her eye. His big hands on the wheel, his sharp jawline and those full lips caused an unwelcome need to stir deep in her belly, a need she hadn't felt for over a year.

She remembered everything: every touch, every erotic whisper, the teasing humor and the arguments over nothing that always ended with his lips on hers. Swallowing hard, Kelly inhaled deeply and turned away, fighting to clear her mind, hoping he couldn't detect her body's traitorous response.

"So," she said, clearing her throat, looking straight ahead, "I can't imagine this tiny spot on the map holding any interest for you. Big celebrity. Small town. Why are you here?"

For a few minutes, she thought he wasn't going to answer her question.

"I needed some downtime," he finally said. "I have a friend who lives in the area, as you know, and this seemed to be as good a place as any."

"You buy an entire ranch to take a break?"

He shrugged.

"And you call me an idiot."

Obviously, he didn't care to share his true intentions with her, which suited her just fine. She should be used to his lies and secrets by now.

"What about you?" he asked.

"What about me?"

"Still in school?"

"No."

So much had happened over the past year his question seemed strange. Her life had changed so radically it felt as though she was answering for someone else. The massive heart attack that had taken her grandfather had been sudden and devastating. Then the bank foreclosed on his farm, leaving Kelly and her younger brother to scramble for another place to live. And just when she thought things couldn't possibly get any worse, she'd discovered she was pregnant by a man who'd hidden his identity, then all but disappeared.

That sobering thought assisted in her return to reality.

"Why did you lie?" It came out a whisper. The question seemed to break free of her mouth, not waiting on her brain to give its permission. "Why did you think it necessary?"

He'd wanted someone to share his bed while here visiting friends. She got that. But why lie about who he was? And why promise to call or come back if he'd known all along he wouldn't?

"What does it matter now?"

"The truth always matters."

"I gave you a name. That should have been enough. If you'd known my true identity it would have made a difference in our relationship."

She stared at him in amazement. "Is it tough carrying around all that arrogance?" She shook her head.

"It's not arrogance," he shot back. "If you'd realized who I was you would have—" He inhaled deeply and blew it out.

"What? I would have what? Not thought of you as Jekyll and Hyde? Not known you would rather climb a tree and tell a lie than stand on the ground and tell the truth? Not felt like I was being played? All of the above?"

"You would have treated me differently." Almost under his breath, he muttered, "They all do. And you were not being played. Ever."

"*They all do?* Who is *they?*"

She saw his hand grip the steering wheel in a tight fist. "What I do for a living had nothing to do with us." He glanced at her through the dim glow on the dash lights. "People hear my name and suddenly they can't see *me*. I should have told you the truth, but I wanted you to know *me*, Kelly. I'm just a man. And I enjoy being seen as one instead of all the damned hype. I intended to explain when I got back here. I intended to tell you the truth."

"Really. Why? If, as you say, a name doesn't matter, why bother?"

She heard him expel a deep sigh. "You're purposely twisting this around."

"I am?"

She heard his huff of frustration.

"We were two people who met and enjoyed being together. At least I enjoyed being with you. Why did it need to be more complicated than that? Or am I missing something?"

Her eyes shot toward him. Had he really said that with a straight face? She couldn't hold back a snort. "You do realize you're trying to justify your deception?" The man wouldn't recognize truth if it smacked him in the face. "Unbelievable." She'd gotten her answer. She should have saved herself the trouble of asking. "At least I provided you and your friends with a good laugh."

Heat rolled up her neck at the thought of his wealthy friends laughing about his affair with a stupid country bumpkin. How easily she'd bought into his deception.

"I never laughed." His tone indicated surprise she would think that. He glanced at her, the hard masculine mouth pulled to a taut line, his eyebrows drown into a frown. "Our relationship wasn't a joke. At least not to me. And I had every intention of coming back and talking to you. I'd hoped you would understand."

"I'm sure you did." The anger rolled off her tongue. "But things happen, right?"

"Yeah. I guess they do. For instance, you never told me which correctional center you were in. Apparently I'm not the only one who can be accused of keeping secrets."

Her head snapped around toward him. *What did he just say?* For several seconds she couldn't speak. Had she heard him correctly? "*What?*"

"I said I—"

She raised her hand, palm side toward him. "Does someone write this stuff for you or do you make it up all by yourself?" He expected her to buy the excuse he hadn't come back because he thought she was in *jail*? She shook her head in amazement. "You really need to seek help."

The man she remembered had clearly changed. She

couldn't help but ask herself which one was the real Jace Compton. "Turn left at the light."

"Left?"

"We live in town now." Jace was remembering her grandfather's small farm.

"Kelly, are you saying you don't have a criminal record?"

"Duhhh. Are you saying you honestly thought I *did*?"

"But—"

"You know what, Jack... Jace—whatever your name is today—just don't say anything else." She'd heard more than enough. "Obviously, you're incapable of being honest. I don't care anymore, all right? I don't care why you lied. I don't care why you never came back. I don't give a rat's behind who you are and I don't want to sit here and listen to your wild excuses. I'm sorry I even brought it up."

Jace didn't speak again, but Kelly felt the anger crackling in the air between them.

The route took them south, toward the low-rent side of town where the small forty-year-old houses marred the landscape and even a fresh coat of paint did little to hide the weathered conditions along the rutted streets. Inside the houses lived people like herself, who worked too hard for too little. But she refused to be embarrassed. The house was old and small, but it was clean. It had a new roof and the amount she paid for rent couldn't be beat. "Third street to the right and down a block. On the right. It's the white house with green shutters."

With her hand on the door handle, Kelly made ready her escape. But by the time they pulled up to the curb and she remembered to unfasten the seat belt, Jace held the door for her, seemingly oblivious to the rain.

Her younger brother stood on the front porch leaning on one of the support posts. The glow of the outside light fanned out over the small front yard.

Jace nodded toward the teen. "How ya doing?"

Kelly watched Matt's body language shift as he recognized Jace. It was clear he was having a hard time believing it. He stared at the big man standing next to the truck.

"You're... Are you? You're Jace Compton!" Matt's eyes were as big as dessert plates as his mouth dropped open in sheer astonishment.

"Matt, go inside," Kelly ordered.

"You want to come in?" Her younger brother totally ignored her request. Anger tinged with fear coursed through her, quickening her steps to the house. This was so not happening. What if Matt had picked up Henry from the sitter?

"No," she stated firmly, and turned back to Jace. "I don't think that's a good idea. Thanks for the ride. It was very... enlightening."

Jace made no reply, just stared at her through the soft glow from the porch light. Kelly hurried to the house. "Matt, get inside." When he didn't move, she snapped, "Now."

"But Kelly—" he looked as though she'd just told him to rob a bank "—do you know who that is?"

The question was almost laughable. Almost.

"Have a good night," Jace called from the curb.

Kelly grabbed Matt by the arm and pulled him inside. At fifteen, her brother already stood a couple of inches taller than her own five foot seven and pulling him anywhere was a challenge. This time, with the adrenaline flowing, she managed. She closed the front door and prepared for the onslaught. She didn't have to wait long.

"I can't believe you." Matt glared in her direction. "*The* Jace Compton at our house and you wouldn't let him come inside. What is your deal? Are you like...crazy?"

"Matt..." There was no way to explain.

"Forget all the movies. He still holds the record for completed passes in the entire NFL. The *record*, Kelly. The guy is a football legend."

Matt lived and breathed football, so she understood what he was saying. But her brother didn't know Jace Compton. Unfortunately, she did.

"Come to think of it—" Matt frowned "—what were you doing in his truck? How did you—?"

"He bought the old Miller spread and had a new house built so Don asked me to clean it. When I finished, the car wouldn't start."

"Jace Compton is living here? In Calico Springs? Like *permanently*?" With each question, Matt's voice rose in excitement. His eyes were wide with elation. He hadn't even taken note of the fact that they had no transportation.

"I really don't know." Kelly didn't want to discuss it. Jace had chosen to keep his reasons for being here to himself, so there was really nothing to tell Matt. She just wanted the man to stay as far away from her small family as possible. "I'm gonna walk down to Mrs. Jenkins's and pick up Henry."

"He's here." Matt was clearly still annoyed, his tone full of frustration. "Mrs. J fed him and got him ready for bed. Football practice was canceled because of the rain so I brought him home."

"Thanks, Matt." She smiled and walked toward the small bedroom she shared with her son. Bless the elderly woman down the street who kept Henry while Kelly worked and who refused to accept one penny for her efforts.

The baby slept in his favorite position, on his tummy, his little butt in the air. Kelly pulled off her wet T-shirt and jeans and grabbed her old robe from the closet. Then, unable to resist, she approached the crib and softly caressed the little head. Sensing his mother's touch, Henry stirred. With a smile, Kelly picked up the sleepy bundle, holding him close, loving the sensation of her tiny son against her heart.

Henry had Jace's dark lashes, even his dimples. Kelly shook her head, still in disbelief that he'd moved here. She should have known Jace would come back to stir up the painful memories it had taken months to overcome. He was no different from her father. Love 'em and leave 'em and not give a damn who he hurt in the process. Move on to the next conquest and never look back. Only this time, the man in question had looked back.

Because of her father's lies and cheating, her mom had taken her own life. That was when dear ole dad had disappeared for good. Kelly had made a pledge then and there that she'd never let a man get close to her. And she'd kept up her resolve. Until Jace. She shook her head at the irony. The one man she'd made the mistake of trusting made her father look like a guppy compared to a twenty-foot shark. And look where it had gotten her.

Forcing the negative thoughts from her mind, she kissed Henry's little head and walked toward the kitchen and the aspirin bottle. Her own head was pounding. After the last hour, she might take two. The very idea that Jace actually believed she'd been in jail was…laughable.

But she wasn't laughing. The man apparently believed his own hype. He really did live in a world of make-believe.

She reached for the aspirin bottle and heard Matt talking to someone in the next room. Curious, she rounded the corner just in time to see Jace Compton step inside the small living room.

Immediate and total panic set into every fiber of her being.

"You, ah, left your purse in the truck." He held the small bag out to her, his eyes glinting wickedly. "Practice makes perfect?"

She glared. She stepped forward and snatched the purse from his hand, and then turned toward the bedroom, hoping he'd go out the same way he came in.

"Kelly?"

She stopped. This was so not happening. Jace walked over to where she stood. His gaze focused on the baby in her arms before those green eyes pinned her to the spot.

"Who do we have here?"

Three

It was here. The moment she'd dreaded since the day Henry was born. She looked down at the baby in her arms, hoping Jace wouldn't see the panic that engulfed her.

"This is Henry," she said and swallowed hard.

"Yours?"

She blinked more than once at his question. Apparently his manager hadn't lied when he'd said he wouldn't tell Jace about the pregnancy. He'd never even told Jace she called.

"Yes," she finally answered. "He's all mine."

Jace looked at her, and then glanced back at the baby. Henry kicked his feet, blowing some of his best baby bubbles for the strange man.

"He's cute," Jace murmured. "How old is he?"

No surprise he would ask. She had to give him an answer. To avoid a reply might only increase his curiosity. "Four months."

She saw the wheels turning in Jace's head as he did the math and knew what conclusion he reached: Henry could be his son. He looked at Kelly again, as though searching for a different answer. His full lips were pulled into a straight line of contemplation.

"I'm Kelly's brother, Matt." Her brother grinned from ear to ear, obviously dying to talk to his hero. Kelly welcomed the interruption.

"Nice to meet you, Matt." That killer grin spread across Jace's face. He held out his hand and Matt shook it. Matt was so excited, it was as if he rose two feet above the ground.

"So Kelly says you're living in Calico Springs now?"

Jace nodded, his eyes shifting toward Kelly for an instant and then back to Matt.

"Yeah. I bought an old ranch north of town. Have a friend who has been in horse racing for thirty years. I always wanted to have land and horses. He talked me into trying my hand at raising some thoroughbreds. There's enough room to bring in some cattle later if I decide to expand."

"Oh man, that's cool." Matt's entire body vibrated in excitement. Matt pointed to a chair. "Can you stay a couple of minutes?"

"Sure."

As they sat down, Matt asked, "Do you still throw a ball?"

"Oh, yeah. Any chance I get." Jace's heart-stopping grin reappeared. "I'd still be a wide receiver if the knee hadn't gotten bent the wrong way. Do you play?"

"Yeah. Well, it's just high school."

"Hey, it's where we all started. What position?"

As the football banter between the two continued, Kelly eased out of the room. She put Henry down in the crib, and then collapsed onto the small wooden chair by the door. When would this day finally end? Jace Compton, the lying, two-faced multimillionaire, was sitting in her living room talking with her brother, probably speculating if he'd just been two feet away from his own son. And from the sound of their animated conversation, the two guys shared a common interest. This was going to get worse before it got better.

She wouldn't think it odd of the Jace she'd met last year. A regular guy. One who fit into the world she knew: a guy who loved cheeseburgers, hot rods and practical jokes. He'd been a decent, down-to-earth guy who'd talked of everyday things. No arrogance. No haughtiness. But it seemed unbelievable the suave wealthy superstar who traveled the globe would sit in an old house and enjoy conversing with a fifteen-year-old kid. It was as though Jace was two different people. In spite of everything, deep inside she still wanted to paint him as a good guy. But she knew he was anything but.

Breathe deep. She'd told no one the identity of Henry's father, not even Matt. Infants didn't resemble either parent enough for someone to see a resemblance. Did they? Most babies had dimples. Maybe she'd get through this.

To her brother, Jace was a true hero, a superstar both in his action films and on the football field. The chance to talk to *the great Jace Compton* one-on-one was beyond exciting. She got that. But she would exercise caution. Usually a fair judge of character, apparently she'd misjudged Jace once. She wouldn't make the same mistake again.

The two voices filled the small space as Kelly grabbed dry clothes and headed for a hot shower. When she emerged some twenty minutes later, all was quiet. She saw the glow under her brother's door and heard the faint sound of music coming from inside. She pulled the air deep into her lungs and blew it out as relief loosened the muscles of her neck and shoulders. Like a major storm that dropped down from the sky without warning, Jace had again breezed in and out, this time leaving no damage behind. But more storms would come. Jace wouldn't let this go. She knew in her gut he hadn't been convinced. He would think about it. Remember their time together. And he would be back.

As Jace drove through the small town square headed north toward the ranch, he couldn't get Kelly and her baby out of his mind. His heart had dropped to his knees when he first saw the infant in her arms. The last thing he'd expected was for Kelly to have a child. Then the idea had hit him hard. *Was he the father?* He'd always been so careful. He didn't want to have any kids. He knew all too well what the title of dad meant in his family.

To this day, he could still vividly remember the smell of

burned grease and scorched onions that had filled every corner of the shoddy apartment above the fast-food joint where he and his parents lived when he was around ten or eleven. It was during that time that something had happened. Something had changed. He never knew what. His mother had refused to discuss any of it. But his father had begun drinking and the arguments between them had grown worse. Louder. More intense. Then the abuse had started, his dad taking his fist to the first one he saw when he walked through the door. To try to protect his mom, Jace had endured a lot of it. His mother had been the strong one, taking her son away from the horrific situation. A couple of times after the divorce, his father had found them and it got bad before the cops arrived. Even after all these years, Jace still hadn't completely let go of his hatred of the man. And he would always admire his mom's strength of will.

Finally, in the predawn hours of a Sunday morning, two police officers had stood outside their door. They'd explained that her ex, George Compton, had been killed in an alley behind a bar. Jace's only thought had been that some stranger got to the bastard before he could.

Jace could still feel the sinking sensation he'd experienced when reality hit that night. In that moment, with those two cops standing at the door, he'd had an epiphany. He was George Compton's son.

He'd never put it into perspective before. His primary focus had always been survival. He and his father shared the same face and deep jaw. They had the same green eyes. Same color hair. If they were so much alike on the outside, it had to be true for the inside. When Jace had realized that, the earth seemed to tilt and spin.

Before he turned sixteen, he'd been in and out of juvie a half dozen times for altercations with guys in the neighborhood and at school who had somehow found out about his dad and wanted to see if the son was as worthless. He'd had so many suspensions he never did figure out how they'd let him stay in school. His junior year, he'd tried out for football on a dare. He put himself up against classmates who had been active in the sport since fifth grade and wanted to see Jace Compton go down. They were merciless on the new kid, which suited Jace just fine. He'd poured out all his aggression on the field. It was his saving grace. And, as it turned out, football was something he was good at. After three games, he'd earned the respect of a lot of his teammates. His grades came up, and just before graduation he was offered a college scholarship. His love of the sport carried him almost four years. Then amazingly he'd been picked up by the pros. No one knew that every tackle he made, he was taking down George Compton. Every catch and subsequent dash for the goalpost was a *screw you* to his old man.

After a freak injury ended his football career, Jace began to work with young athletes. He enjoyed teaching them about his favorite sport anytime he got the chance. But any hope that he'd someday have kids and a family of his own had been stomped into the ground a long time ago, beaten out of him by his father's fists.

Still, the idea of Kelly bearing his son was immediately, unbelievably gratifying. His body surged to readiness. Protective instincts rallied to the surface, taking him to a place he'd never been before.

He took a deep breath, pulling the humid night air into his lungs. If the child was his, why hadn't Kelly called? He knew instinctively she wouldn't have kept something so important from him. It wasn't her way. And surely she would want help with the baby, child support...*something*. Most women would beat a path to their attorney as soon as a pregnancy was confirmed. There had been two women who had actually schemed to make Jace think they were pregnant just to get rings on their fingers or obtain a few million dollars in their bank accounts.

But Kelly wasn't like other women. He would be wise to

keep that in mind. It wasn't only her beauty that drew him to her. She was feisty and independent to a fault. She was intelligent and decisively stubborn. Her convictions and beliefs ran deep, and her sense of right and wrong went to the core.

What phone number had he given her before he left? He couldn't remember. The security he had to maintain made it damn near impossible to reach him by phone unless one knew the phrase or identifying password. It changed every few weeks. Had he provided his private cell number? His gut tightened. If she'd tried to call when she realized she was expecting and couldn't get through his security, she would be…furious. Suddenly all the little pieces fell into place with the force and impact of a nuclear implosion.

Dammit to hell.

He slammed on the brakes, bringing the truck to a screeching stop. Jerking it into reverse, he backed into a side street, turned around and headed back to Kelly's house. No wonder she'd wanted to get away from him and been so angry. Not only had he lied to her, but he'd gotten her pregnant and left the country. Then the first time he saw her in over a year he'd called her a crook.

Jace wanted to punch something other than a punching bag. Bret better be glad he was a thousand miles away. Jace had zero doubt his manager had lied to keep Jace from coming back to her. That he'd ever bought into that crap about Kelly having a criminal record caused a giant ball of rage to churn in his gut. His instincts had told him not to believe Bret at the time. Why the hell hadn't he listened to them? Bret probably saw her as a threat to his future income. If Jace quit the films, his manager's gravy-train run would be over.

But while it was easy enough to blame his manager, ultimately, in this, there was no one to blame but himself.

His mind returned to Kelly. A thousand questions hit him with pinpoint accuracy and he couldn't answer even one of them. Did he have a child? A son? Despite using precautionary measures, it was more than possible. When he'd held Kelly in his arms, the passion was intense beyond anything he'd ever experienced. He'd never wanted to let her go. His desire for her was insatiable. Their nights together had turned into days, and then back into nights. It began as hot sexual need. But by the time he had to leave, that white-hot passion had expanded into the blending of two souls. Even now, just thinking about her, those blue-green eyes crazy with need for him, the scent of her shampoo, the feel of her silky skin and the soft cries as her desire crested at the pinnacle of their lovemaking, had parts of him hard and throbbing. Kelly had a way of making him crazy. Apparently some things didn't change.

Kelly sighed with relief knowing she'd skirted one confrontation, but was equally aware there would be more to come. Jace wouldn't give up and just go away. She knew him that well. He went at everything he did with dogged determination. Whether it was training a filly at the ranch where he'd stayed a year ago or hiding his identity from the world. From her. While it had been a shock to learn his real name and profession, it didn't come as a surprise how easily he'd duped her. Jace Compton was proficient at anything he set out to do. It was small wonder he was highly acclaimed as an actor. And according to Matt, Jace had received the same admiration when he played pro football. It was all or nothing. *Defeat* wasn't a word in his vocabulary.

But she qualified the thought: it was possible he hadn't as yet come up against a mother protecting her child. Whatever rules governed his life would fly out the window. There were no offsides or penalties. No interceptions. No retakes. Kelly might not be a match for him on a football field or a movie set, but Jace would encounter significant resistance if he tried to push into her life with intentions of taking her child. Figuratively, he'd be lucky if he came out with only minor scratches and a limp.

She'd just turned off the kitchen light and was headed to her bedroom when a hard knock on the front door stopped her in her tracks. *Surely not.* Surely Jace wouldn't come back here tonight. But intuition told her he was standing on the porch. Squaring her shoulders, she returned to the front room and opened the door.

"We need to talk."

It was neither a demand nor a question, but somewhere in between. She wasn't about to act as though she didn't know what he wanted to discuss. With a glance back at Matt's closed door, she stepped outside, closing the front door behind her. She absently noticed the rain had stopped. A cooling breeze touched her skin. Somewhere in the distance crickets chirped. But her focus was on the big man who stood in front of her, almost a silhouette in the night.

"Is the baby mine?"

Kelly wanted to be anywhere but here. She had often envisioned this moment, but at the same time kidded herself into believing it would never happen. She drew in a deep breath. She couldn't lie to a man about his own child. Regardless of what he'd done to her, he had the right to know the truth. It was what he might try to do with that truth that had her on the brink of panic.

"Yes."

"Kelly, why didn't you tell me? The cell number I gave you should have worked."

He didn't question whether she was telling the truth, a fact that surprised her. But his voice held frustration mixed with anger. She knew only too well what those feelings felt like.

As many times and in as many ways as she'd tried and failed to reach him, his question sounded ridiculous. Part of her wanted to go back inside the house and close the door behind her, refusing to give him a second more of her time. The other part of her wanted to share the wonder of their beautiful son. The little things that made him laugh.

The way he mouthed what would someday be words. The overall amazement of him.

Did Jace deserve to know such things? Did he even care? She'd wasted months of her life alternately wishing he would come back and hoping he never would. In her mind she'd practiced what she would say if she ever saw him again, all sorts of scenarios with a wide variety of outcomes. Now that the moment was here, she didn't have a clue how to proceed or what to say. She crossed her arms over her chest and faced him.

"I did try to reach you. It was a bit of a challenge since I didn't even know your name."

"Kelly—" He raked his hand through his hair.

"The cell number you gave me kicked over to a voice mail box that was full. You really should learn to delete your old messages. Some new ones might be important."

She'd swear he cringed.

"I was able to contact your friend, Garret. The son of the rancher you stayed with last year? He gave me another number and a password, but apparently he had it wrong or it had been disconnected.

"I did speak with your manager. Bret… Gold-something. Goldberg? Goldman? Is that right? It took me about a week to track him down. Another five weeks to get him on the phone. He didn't think it was such a good idea that I talk with you."

She ignored the obscenities that fell from Jace's mouth.

"I tried a couple more times to reach you through your cell, but after a few months, I gave up. So. Now you know. You have a son. Belated congratulations."

Kelly could hear the sarcasm in her own voice but made no effort to conceal it.

"Kelly… I screwed up, okay?"

She shook her head. "No, you didn't. Screwing up is when you do something accidentally. Not when it's done on purpose. And so, no. In this case, it isn't okay. You lied.

You lied to me from the moment we met. Then you disappeared and never looked back."

How many nights had she lain in bed, consumed with the need to hold him, to touch him, to hear his voice again? At times the want had been almost unbearable, her mind elevating it to the level of death. Had he ever thought of her? Did he even remember any part of their time together?

She could sense his aura now, feel the warmth from his body through the darkness, and that same need ran through her like liquid fire. What was it about this man that made her want to forget the past year? Just forget everything and step into his arms and feel his touch once again? The thought made her angry, and she held on to that emotion. She couldn't be weak. She had to think of Henry and be strong.

"I understand why you're mad. You have every right to be."

"Yes. I do. And before you accuse me of getting pregnant on purpose, I didn't. I had a career plan and had envisioned a vastly different future. I have no way to prove it and I don't intend to try. Now, did you want anything else? Or are we finished?"

"I...I don't know. I've only known I had a son for two minutes."

"Give it about nine months. Maybe it will soak in." She hesitated, looking absently at the worn paint on the porch where they stood. "He...he almost died, you know?" Her voice broke; tears burned her eyes. "When he was born? They thought I would lose him. For six days, it was hour to hour, minute to minute. But he's a tough little guy. He may not have been expected or wanted but... Yeah. He's strong. And he's smart." She quickly swiped the tears from her cheeks. "If he gets his strength from his father, I'm grateful to you for that."

"I want to take care of you. Both of you."

Logic demanded she consider if it was fair to Henry to

deny the financial assistance Jace was more than capable of providing. But they were doing okay. Henry wanted for nothing and she didn't want to open Pandora's Box. She shook her head. "We don't need to be *taken care of.* I want nothing from you. And he doesn't need anything from you. There are no shackles here. Contrary to popular belief, I've never tried to con anyone. Or entrap them. I'm not about to start now. So just…you know, carry on with your life. Throw your wild parties. Make your films. It's a little late for regrets, so don't give us a second thought. We'll be fine."

It took a long time before he could swallow the huge wedge of emotion caught in his throat. Jace couldn't let it end this way. In light of this new overwhelming discovery that he had a son, he instantly thought of his own upbringing and the monster it had made of him. For now it lay dormant inside, but eventually it would awaken. He should distance himself from Kelly and the baby. But his heart throbbed with the idea they had a son. They'd created a child. *He was a father.* That, in itself, was enough to mess up any man's mind. And regardless of how hard he fought to hold on, his common sense went down the tubes.

"I want to be in his life." The words fell from his lips as though he was determined to be heard regardless of the consequences.

"Then what?" She shrugged. "Get your attorneys involved? Let them decide on a visitation schedule that meets with your own agenda? See him when you have time or when you happen to be in the country? Introduce him to all your lady friends vying to be his new mommy? Let him grow up seeing his dad's face on TV or the big screen? I'm sure the other kids will someday envy him for that. Wow." Her sarcasm was obvious. "Maybe have your secretary send an expensive gift on his birthday? That's always a nice touch."

"Dammit, Kelly. I don't know how to answer you. I

haven't had a chance to work anything out." He held her gaze as though it was a lifeline while experiencing a rush of emotions he didn't want to feel and had no clue how to deal with.

"Then let me answer the questions for you. No. No to you seeing him once or twice a year. No to long-distance phone calls and the inevitable excuses when you miss his birthday. Or his first spelling bee. Or his first softball game. No to him being a media spectacle. He deserves more, and I won't step aside and let you do that to him. Somehow I'll stop you if you try."

He ran a hand over his face. *Dammit.* He couldn't deny that a lot of what she said was true. She'd pretty much nailed what would happen if his life continued as it had for the past twelve years. He was more than ready for some normal in his crazy life. He wanted a home, a family. But he didn't know how to change, and if he was honest with himself, he didn't know if he wanted to. The work, the travel, the physical aspects of it, the concentration needed…it was the only thing keeping the monster inside at bay.

It was a damned if you do, damned if you don't situation. He should take the out she was offering, make sure Kelly had plenty of money in her bank account and leave them both alone before he caused them to be thrown into the media spotlight, which she would no doubt view as under the bus. Before he became abusive like his old man. It made Jace every kind of selfish for wanting to keep them in his life. But he did. And how convoluted was that?

Despite her show of bravado, he wanted to pull her into his arms, hold her close and promise he would make everything okay. But he couldn't. He didn't know how to make her believe things would work out when he had doubts about it himself. He knew he had to do *something*. But the answer of how to make this right seemed worlds away.

After all she'd been through Kelly had more internal fortitude than anyone he'd ever known, with the single exception of his mom. But while Kelly's resilience and internal strength were admirable, he couldn't leave things as they were regardless of what she said she wanted or, in fact, didn't want.

"He is my son."

"Yes." She nodded. "He is."

"And you want me to just walk away?"

She looked down, as though giving her answer serious thought. "I'm telling you that you have a choice. His life will not revolve around yours. I won't stand by while you break his heart, then try and pick up the pieces after you again disappear."

"Kelly—"

She raised her hand to silence him.

"That said…" She hesitated as if making up her mind about a difficult decision. "I have plans for tomorrow, but if you want to see him while you're here, come by Monday afternoon. I get home around five thirty. He's still too young to form any attachment or be upset when you leave." She again brushed at a spot just below her eye. He heard a soft sniff. "I'm not doing this to be mean, Jace. You have every right to see your son. He's beautiful. You will be so proud. I…I wish you could be in his life always. Every day. But we both know that isn't realistic. And I have to protect Henry, even if it's from his own father."

"We can work this out, Kelly. I know we can."

Her eyes found his through the darkness. "Maybe," she whispered.

Maybe was better than *no*. Jace would take it for the time being. He understood what she was saying. Between the travel his career required and the fear that he might someday become as abusive as his father, he couldn't argue—even though he wanted to.

"I have to be up early in the morning. It's late."

"Okay. Monday. Five thirty. I'll see you then."

Kelly nodded, stepped inside and closed the door.

* * *

Jace blindly turned and walked to his truck. His emotions were all over the place. Even though he didn't like it at all, he had to give merit to Kelly's need to protect the baby. He wanted to be angry with her, his mind playing out the possibilities of what would have happened if he hadn't come back. Would she have waited until the child was grown to introduce them? Or simply raised the boy to believe he had no father? Either way was unacceptable. Yet on the heels of that thought was the fact that she had tried to reach him. He had no doubt she'd tried. It was a vicious circle and it all came back to him. He'd screwed up. Royally.

He climbed inside the truck, slamming the door quite a bit harder than was needed. All the regrets, all the shouldas and couldas, were tripping through his mind. But the big question was: what was he going to do now? It was so overwhelming he wished he had reason to doubt his paternity. But he knew, without any doubt, the baby was his. Kelly just wasn't a person who would make up something like this. Some would. But not Kelly.

Inasmuch as she intended her life to continue as it had so far, Jace knew it wouldn't happen. Her world was about to change and, from her perspective, not necessarily for the better. Sooner or later the media would find out about the ranch. It was only a matter of time. And eventually there was a very good possibility they would discover Kelly and their son. Especially if she'd listed Jace's name on the birth certificate. It would turn her life into a media circus, one she was not equipped to handle. He'd dealt with overzealous fans many times and knew what they were capable of. It wouldn't be safe for Kelly or the baby, and he could not stand back and let that happen.

He pulled away from the curb and headed for the ranch. *He had a son.* Even knowing all the obstacles in front of them, the idea of having a child was enthralling. The more the fact soaked in, the more incredible it became.

How could he go forward and not include Kelly and the baby in his life? Her vulnerability, her innocence about the world and the people in it who would use her for a stepping-stone to further their career, concerned him. The overwhelming desire to take care of her and the baby fought the knowledge that it could never happen because someday he could hurt them. A surge of intense feelings for her made him ache inside. The war that raged was the most intense pain he'd ever experienced. Broken bones had nothing on the anguish tearing his insides to shreds.

If he cared about Kelly, about his son, he needed to walk away. But where would he find the strength to do so?

Four

"Thanks so much for the ride, Gerri," Kelly told her friend as together they walked through the outside glass doors and down the steps of Great West Insurance. "I really do appreciate it."

"Not a problem, ever. You know that."

Kelly still hadn't found anyone to check out her car. With fall roundup in full swing, all the guys she knew had either signed on as ranch hands for the extra wages or had something else going on. The local garage had offered to send someone out, but wanted one hundred and fifty dollars just to make the trip to Jace's ranch. She'd told the mechanic she'd have to get back with him, biting her tongue to keep from calling him a crook.

The car had been on her mind constantly since she'd left Jace's home two days ago. Knowing it still sat on his property was unsettling; it was a tie to him she didn't want.

But as they turned onto her street, Kelly had to blink twice. Her old car sat in the driveway, and parked next to the curb was Jace's dark metallic-blue pickup.

"Hey, Kelly," Gerri said. "Looks like someone decided to help you out after all."

When Gerri pulled up behind the truck, Kelly saw Matt and Jace tossing a football across the expanse of three front yards.

"Yeah. Maybe. I'll see you tomorrow. Thanks again."

Kelly walked toward Mrs. Jenkins's house, hoping Gerri would drive away. Thankfully, she did, sticking her hand out the open window to wave goodbye as the Toyota continued down the street.

Mrs. Jenkins's home was only two houses down and around the corner. She was lucky to have such a kind and loving woman to keep the baby while she worked. Mrs. Jenkins's family had moved to another state the previous year and she longed for her own children and grandchildren. She'd assured Kelly that keeping Henry was a joy. It filled a void in her life. It was a great solution for all concerned.

Returning to her house with Henry, Kelly had just set the baby bag on the sofa and still had Henry in her arms when she saw Jace walking toward the door. Her heart immediately began doing flip-flops. Even the warmth of the baby snuggled against her couldn't make her relax. What she wouldn't give for Jace to be a regular person with a normal job. Maybe then things would have turned out differently. But why waste her time wishing for something that wasn't even in the realm of possibility? She didn't want to keep Jace from his son. But at the same time, his father's world was not a place the baby should be.

As soon as Jace spotted her standing behind the screen door with the baby in her arms, that infamous smile spread across his face. Kelly pushed open the door and bade him to enter. Gingerly, Jace reached out and touched Henry's hand. The baby laughed and grabbed the offered finger, kicking his feet in excitement.

"Hi, buddy." The acceptance was immediate. Apparently on both sides. "He's amazing."

"Would you like to hold him?"

Jace nodded, his eyes switching from Kelly to the baby, then back to Kelly. A twinge of heat surged through her body. Jace was so masculine, so totally male, every hormone she had was screaming to get closer. It was unsettling. His earthy aroma swirled around her, and she swallowed hard.

"Take a seat," she offered, clearing her throat, then placed the little bundle in his father's arms. Henry looked so tiny, and Jace looked so awkward, so out of place, but she couldn't miss the look of pride in his handsome features. As she silently watched father and son interact for the first time, she couldn't help but ask herself how Jace could look even sexier when he held the baby. His tanned arms and dark features were such a contrast to Henry's pale skin and hair. The sheer sexuality rolled off him in waves. So male. So powerful. So compelling. She ran the fingers of one hand through her hair in an effort to regain control of her wayward thoughts.

"He's just starting to respond to voices and smiles. He can almost roll over from his tummy onto his back. One day soon I'll go in the bedroom and find him trying to pull up and stand. His pediatrician said he is exceptional in both his mental and physical development."

Jace nodded, still staring at the baby as if he were in a trance. Kelly knew the feeling. The first time she'd been allowed to hold her son, she'd been captivated. A miniature of his father, complete with dimples, Henry was going to be a heartbreaker someday.

Just like his dad.

While Jace held his son, speaking softly to him and chuckling at his antics, Kelly eased into the kitchen and took her cell phone from her purse. Bringing up the camera, she returned to the living room and clicked away. This was a memorable moment for all three of them.

"If you'll give me your email address, I'll send them to you."

"Thanks, Kelly," Jace said in a tone that indicated he really did appreciate the gesture.

She returned to the chair and sat down.

"Tell me more about him."

She shrugged. Where to begin? "He's a happy baby. He loves the water and bath time. He has a small yellow plastic duck he will try and grab. His efforts send water splashing in every direction and it makes him laugh, so he splashes some more. My coworkers bought him a little swing. You wind it up and it will stay in motion about half an hour. Henry loves that, too."

"How did you choose his name?"

"Henry was my grandfather's name."

Jace nodded.

"His...his middle name is Jason."

Jace's head shot up and that green gaze held hers. "You named him after me?"

Kelly shrugged. "It seemed like the right thing to do." The warmth of a blush touched her cheeks as the glint of surprise and obvious happiness showed in his eyes. "I've started reading to him. Of course he doesn't understand what I'm saying, but he seems to like it."

"He responds to the sound of your voice." Jace looked at her. "Like father, like son."

For an instant their eyes met and held. Kelly swallowed hard, fighting against a sudden overwhelming sense of loss. It felt as though somebody had reached in and ripped out everything inside. Which was crazy. How long would this man have such a compelling effect on her? His voice had always sent shivers across her skin, and now was no different. She remembered lying on the blanket under the shade of a giant oak tree, her head resting on his muscled chest, held close and protected in his heavy arms. She remembered how good just being in his presence had made her feel.

Pushing away those memories, Kelly continued to share small things about Henry's life. She kept her gaze locked on the baby. She didn't need any more remembrances of Jace distracting her. The recollections she'd managed to bury could stay buried. Feeling his arms around her again would never happen. The past was best left in the past.

Eventually their quiet conversation lulled the baby to sleep. Kelly took him from Jace and put him in his crib, covering him with his blue puppy blanket. When she returned Jace was standing at the front door.

"Do I have you to thank for getting my car home?"

He shrugged those broad shoulders. "No big deal."

"I called everyone I knew and no one had time to look at it." She felt the need to assure him she'd tried to get the car out of his way. "How much do I owe you?"

He shook his head and shrugged. "I just turned the key. You must have given it too much gas and flooded the engine. Desperation for a quick getaway sometimes causes that to happen."

She ignored the gibe. "Well, thank you."

"No problem." He hesitated. "I'd like to invite Matt out to the ranch to throw some footballs. Maybe I can give him some pointers."

"He would love that. He is so into football, and as you will soon discover if you haven't already, you're his hero. But Jace, don't do it because you feel in any way obligated. Eventually, Matt would figure it out and—"

"Gotcha. No worries there. He seems like a good kid. My mom will be staying at the ranch but won't be here for a few days, so tossing the ball with Matt will be great. Brings back the good old days." He grinned and pushed open the door as Matt came jogging up to the porch. "It gets dark around nine. I'll have him home about then."

The afternoon visits and the ball practice with Matt at the ranch became everyday events. Over the next two weeks, Kelly's anger and resentment slowly began to wane to a controllable level. It was so odd having Jace back in her life. Every day she expected him to not show up. But he hadn't missed a day yet. Initially she'd had some sleepless nights, her mind trying to answer the big question: What now? Where was this going? What was he eventually going to do? Did his plans include an attempt to take Henry?

Jace was a brief moment in her past. He had no part in her future other than being her son's father. Never again would she be back in his arms. Ever.

Pushing open the heavy glass door of the insurance company where she worked as assistant customer service rep, Kelly headed toward the side of the building and the employee parking lot. It had been a long day. But it helped keep her mind focused, leaving no time to think about Jace.

Most of the time.

Rounding the outside corner of the building, heading toward the parking lot, she immediately spotted the very subject of her thoughts leaning against her car, his arms crossed over his broad chest. Her heart skipped a beat. Her determination to keep their past where it belonged was an ongoing battle, and every time she saw him, it grew more difficult.

Inside she was jumble of nerves, wanting him to stay away yet missing him, then hating herself for it. Every time a dark blue truck passed, she had to look to see if it was him. When told she had an incoming call at work, she anxiously picked up the receiver, prepared to hear his deep voice on the other end. Errands around town had her searching the faces in the crowd for him.

Now the pulse surged through her veins as she took in the sight of him, and her mind rushed to figure out why he was here.

"Do you have a minute?" he asked when she reached the car.

Kelly shrugged.

Jace hesitated, as though looking for the right words. "I received a phone call about an hour ago. A friend in the media owes me a couple of favors. He called to let me know someone found out I'm the primary stockholder in a company that recently bought a ranch in Calico Springs, Texas. The news media will probably be staking out the ranch by this evening or soon after. Reporters can be ruthless. They can dig up facts you thought were long buried."

Why was he telling her this? This didn't concern her. And if the media discovered Henry was Jace's son, she couldn't stop it.

"So, why tell me? It's not any of my business."

"I'm afraid it might be only a matter of time until they find out about Henry."

"Are you asking me to deny Henry is your son if anyone should inquire? Sorry if he's an embarrassment for you." She adjusted the strap of her purse on her shoulder. "Excuse me. You're blocking the door. I need to get home."

Jace didn't move.

"That's not what I'm saying at all. Kelly, other than his middle name, did you put my name on his birth certificate? As the father?"

She nodded.

"If anyone finds out about Henry, this will blow up into a very big deal. You won't be safe, or at the least, you will be surrounded by the press. Night and day. Everywhere you go. They will follow you to work. They will find out who keeps the baby during the day and do what they have to in order to get a picture. They could even go to Matt's school."

Jace had to see the skepticism on her face. "So…I'll just tell them to leave my property," she countered. "And once the school year begins they should be able to keep any stranger, reporter or not, away from Matt. I mean, they can't just—"

"They can and they will."

"No." She gritted her teeth to keep her anger in check. "No. This will not happen. Dammit, Jace. Keep your media mania on your side of the street and leave my side alone. This was exactly what I told you I didn't want to happen to Henry."

"I know. And I'm sorry. I'd change it if I could."

"So what's the answer? Why are you telling me all of this if there is no way to stop it?"

"You and Henry and Matt need to move out to the ranch as soon as possible."

Her eyebrows shot straight up as she looked at him with

open disbelief. "Yeah. Right. That is so not going to happen."

"Kelly, you're not equipped to deal with this on your own. I have a full security staff in place 24/7." Jace glanced toward a black sedan parked across the street and nodded. The man behind the wheel nodded back.

"You've got to be kidding." He had to be. "Jace, you're blowing this way out of proportion. This is Calico Springs, population six thousand and two. It isn't Los Angeles. It's a quiet little ranching community. Things like you're describing just don't happen here. Now if you'll please step aside, I really need to go and pick up Henry."

With a muttered curse, Jace moved toward the front of the car and opened the door for her. Kelly didn't hesitate to throw her purse onto the passenger seat and slip behind the wheel.

"Take this." He handed her a cell phone. "Just punch Call. There are only three people who will answer it—a couple of my security team and me. If you get into trouble, change your mind or need to reach me, use it."

This was taking on the ambiance of a James Bond thriller. "Are you kidding me?"

Jace looked down at her and shook his head. He wasn't smiling. A small trickle of fear ran down her spine. She took the phone and slipped it into the side pouch of her purse. It seemed easier than arguing about it.

"I won't be coming back in the afternoons. There's too much of a risk someone will see me. Kelly, I really do wish you would—"

"We'll be fine." She turned on the ignition and put the car into reverse. "I'll let Matt know you won't be stopping by for a while."

Jace didn't nod. He said nothing more. He stood in the same spot as she backed out of the parking space and turned toward home.

It must be tough to live your life always looking over

your shoulder. In a way she found it sad. To become so successful in your chosen career that you actually become a target of the very people you sought to entertain. But it was a life he'd chosen. Consequently, he had to deal with the repercussions. It didn't mean she had to.

Five

An unfamiliar sound woke Kelly from her sleep. Frowning, she rubbed her eyes and listened more intently. It sounded like people talking outside her house. She threw the covers back and rolled out of bed. It was early morning, still not completely light. She checked on Henry and adjusted his blanket. He'd slept through the night, so he would be ready for his breakfast soon.

Without bothering to turn on a light, she headed toward the living room, literally bumping into Matt in the hallway.

"Do you hear that?" It took a major shakedown every morning to get Matt to even open his eyes. For him to be awake at this hour...

"Yeah. I heard it."

"What is it?"

"I'm not sure." Separating the blinds just enough to see, they both looked out the front windows. In the predawn light, Kelly saw people. About a dozen of them. And cars and vans lining both sides of the street.

"What's going on, Kelly?" Before she could speak, Matt added, "I'm going out and see what's happening."

"No! Matt. Don't go outside."

In the ever-increasing light Kelly now saw the cameras and the white vans with satellite antennas on top. People were talking among themselves, calling out instructions to their crews. Large black power cords lay over the ground. She swallowed hard. Jace had told her the truth. Anger flared that he had brought this madness to their family, but it was temporarily pushed aside by concern for Henry and Matt.

"Matt, go get dressed and ready for school. You can't be late the second day. Find something to eat for breakfast. There are waffles in the freezer. Fresh fruit in the bowl on the table."

"This is wild." His eyes were as wide as saucers. "Those are reporters, right? Is all this because Jace comes here to visit?"

"No. Not exactly." She didn't know how her brother would take the news, but it was time he was told. Before he heard it on television. "This is because Henry is Jace's son."

Matt's jaw hung open; his eyes went ever wider. "*What?* Oh, man. Are you kidding me? You had a thing with Jace and you never told me? When? How? Where? Are you serious?"

Kelly nodded. "Yes. But it's...complicated. And we don't have time to discuss it now."

"Does Jace know?"

Kelly rubbed her temples. "Yes."

"Henry is Jace Compton's *son*?"

Clearly Matt was struggling with this truth.

"So that's why he invited me out to his place to throw the ball."

Wow. Left field. His disappointment was obvious. "No. Absolutely not. You guys share a love of football and the two of you seemed to...click. He thinks the world of you, Matt. I would never lie about that. He's told me so on more than one occasion." The very last thing she wanted to add to this insanity was hurt feelings. She'd told Matt the truth. She just hoped he would believe it.

Matt was silent for a few worrying seconds. "Okay," he nodded. "Okay. Good. That's cool." The side of his mouth drew up in a half grin and he looked squarely at his sister. "I guess I'm not the only one in this family he *clicked* with."

She felt the heated blush cover her neck and face. Her

eyes narrowed into a glare. "Right now, Matthew Douglas Michaels, I would advise you not to go there. Go get dressed."

Matt headed for his bedroom, a wide grin across his face. His body language was decidedly springy with a bit of teenage swagger thrown in. He was on the *ins* with a superstar. And no doubt he thought he had something on her, as well. From the number of people standing outside their house, he would have to get in line.

With Henry changed and dressed, she went into the kitchen to ready his food. Her purse was on the kitchen table and the cell phone Jace had given her began to ring. When she pulled it out of her bag, she saw there had been numerous calls. She'd never heard it.

"Hello?"

"Why in the hell haven't you answered your phone?" Jace bellowed out, his frustration obvious. "I've been trying to reach you for thirty minutes. Are you all right? Is Henry—?"

"Henry is fine. We're all fine. There are some people outside. They have cameras. I guess you were right. It appears the media found us."

She heard him take a deep breath and blow it out. Kelly couldn't remember Jace ever getting angry or upset about anything. Clearly he was experiencing some anxiety now. Did he actually think something was going to happen to them in Calico Springs?

"Stay in the house. Keep the doors locked. Tom Stanton, my head of security, just arrived and is standing by outside your house. Let us know when you're ready and he'll bring you guys to the ranch and we—"

"Jace, no. I'm not coming to your ranch. I thought I made that clear. I've got to go to work and Matt has to be in school—" she switched Henry to her other arm and checked her watch "—in twenty minutes. I need to take the baby to the sitter's, then be on my way."

"Kelly, I don't think that would be——"

"Please don't waste either of our time telling me you don't think it's a good idea. If you want to help us, we need to get Henry safely to the babysitter and Matt to school."

A prolonged silence met her statement. "Kelly, you can't go on expecting your life to stay the way it was. I'm sorry, honey."

She heard the sincerity in his tone. His endearment made her heart beat a bit faster, her breathing become shallow. His rich baritone voice calling her honey caused a memory to flash in her mind. Jace's arms around her, his hand covering hers as she gripped the end of a fishing pole. They'd been on the edge of a clear blue pond located in an area of the ranch where he'd stayed last year. It had felt as if they were the only two people on earth. Jace had removed his shirt and shoes, leaving only the well-worn, slightly ripped jeans. She'd had a two-pound bass on the line, the first fish she'd ever caught. When it broke the surface of the water, bending and flouncing in an effort to get free of the hook, she hadn't been able to contain the screams of excitement. And she couldn't forget Jace's laughter at her animated enthusiasm. Then the fish had fallen back into the water and seconds later the line went slack. She'd lost it. Jace had hugged her close and murmured, "I'm sorry, honey. Let's see if we can catch him again." But as she'd turned into his arms the fish was forgotten. The soft rays of the summer sun had been joined by the hot sparkle of desire in his eyes and the burning of his hungry lips.

Would she ever be immune to him? To his voice? His touch? How much longer until she could stop having to fight her own body in order to maintain some small amount of control? Kelly brushed the hair back from her face, striving for practicality. She didn't need to turn into one of Jace Compton's groupies, and the past had shown her that was the most she could ever be.

"Kelly? Are you there?"

"Uh...yeah. Yeah. Jace, I can't walk away from my life. Apparently, you can't walk away from yours, either. Matt has to go to school and I need to get dressed and go to work." Why couldn't he understand? Had he been living the high life so long he could no longer relate to ordinary people living ordinary lives?

He finally agreed, but she could tell by his tone he didn't like it. "I'll have Tom send two men to the front door. Tell them where you want to go."

Three days later the craziness had not subsided and her cell phone wouldn't stop ringing. There was no sign the media were giving up. Not only had they increased their ranks, they had been joined by some of the town's residents, their own curiosity compelling them to be part of the excitement. There were what appeared to be tailgate parties going on just past her driveway as far down the street as she could see in both directions, with dozens of lawn chairs lining the yards on both sides. Her home had become a freak show. For the first time in her life, Kelly felt claustrophobia stir her anger.

The switchboard at work had been bombarded with calls since that first day, overwhelming the phone lines. Just after lunch today she'd had a rather unpleasant one-on-one with her boss, who'd recommended she take off early, adding she had a week of vacation and suggested she use it until she got her life in some semblance of order. And now, apparently, her cell number had been discovered and passed out, free for the taking.

Every day, Jace's security team picked Matt up and escorted him home. He was having a great time with all the excitement, enjoying the sudden popularity and inspiring the envy of his classmates, which only added to her growing frustration.

Pacing around the small house, her mind was filled with murderous thoughts, and all of them revolved around Jace.

How could he do this? And why wouldn't he stop it? *I want to be in your life*, he'd said. Ha! What a joke. This media mania was exactly what she'd wanted to avoid. How dare he dump this on her front doorstep?

The cell phone Jace had provided began to ring.

"Hello?"

"Ms. Michaels, this is Tom Stanton of Jace's security detail. Would you like your mail?"

"My *mail*?" Why not? What else did she have to do? "Yeah. Sure."

"One of our men will deliver it to your back door in two minutes."

"Thanks." It seemed as if they were going to a lot of trouble. She mostly received advertisements addressed to "resident," which immediately went into the trash.

At the man's knock, Kelly opened the door. With a respectful nod, he brought in her mail. Three large bags of it.

"What...? What is all this?"

"They're all addressed to you. Probably fan letters."

"*Fan letters?*" Was he kidding?

By the time Matt got home, Kelly was just about to open the second bag. Sitting on the living room floor with Henry playing on a thick blanket next to her, she'd spent the past three hours reading pure crazy.

"You know," Matt said as he walked to where she sat, "we should sell popcorn to those people outside. Make some money off this. What are you doing?" Frowning, he dumped his books onto the sofa. "What is all this?"

"Fan letters." She didn't look up, but she could feel Matt's surprise mixed with excitement from four feet away. "Have a seat. I wouldn't want you to miss one second of this *wonderful* experience."

Ignoring her sarcasm, Matt quickly found a place on the floor and pulled a handful of letters out of the newly opened bag.

"Ha!" Matt laughed. "This girl wants to have Jace's baby

but is happy for you in spite of you beating her to it." He picked up another and began reading.

"Kelly?"

She noticed his face narrow into a serious frown. "You'd better take a look at this." He handed the page to her.

The letter was filled with alarming descriptions of what they intended to do to Kelly and the baby. Off-the-wall acts of violence directed at her and Henry. She felt the blood leave her face as she realized the implications. Suddenly a crashing sound from the bedroom made her jump. It sounded as if a vase had shattered. "Matt, stay with Henry."

Kelly scrambled to her feet and hurried in that direction.

"Sorry about your vase." A woman about her age was standing inside the bedroom, looking around.

"Who are you? How did you get inside my house?" Kelly's voice was about three octaves higher than normal.

The woman shrugged and looked toward the bed. "Through the window. Is that where Jace Compton sleeps?" She spoke as though she was in a daze, as if she'd just stumbled into Neverland. The woman walked over to the bed, smoothed her hands over the covers, and then proceeded to crawl on top of the mattress.

"What are you doing? Get off my bed!"

"It's so soft," the woman said, completely ignoring Kelly's angry demand. "Wow."

Kelly ran for kitchen table and the phone Jace had provided. Her call was immediately answered.

"There is someone in my bedroom." She could hear the anger in her own voice. "She said she climbed in through the window. She's *in* my bed and refuses to leave."

The line went dead and within seconds men were coming in every door to her small house, guns drawn, with Tom Stanton leading the charge. The woman was seized and handcuffed. Notification of the break-in was called into the police, all handled in a practiced and flawless manner by the men in Jace's security detail.

Kelly went back to the front room and picked up Henry. Matt stood next to her, not saying a word.

"The police will need a statement, Ms. Michaels. They should be here any minute."

Kelly nodded and sat down on the sofa, holding Henry close.

"I think you need to see this." Matt shoved a letter into Tom's hand.

"Where did you get this, son?" Tom frowned.

"In the mail. We were reading all this mail." He gestured to letters spread over the floor and one of the bags, still partially full, next to the sofa. "Most of them are stupid. But this one…"

Tom took out his phone and punched a number before turning and walking out of the room. Kelly could hear his voice. She couldn't understand what he said or who he was talking to.

But she had a pretty good idea.

Six

It took Jace most of the drive from the ranch to Kelly's house to bring his temper under a small bit of control. Tom's phone call had his heart racing, his fear for their safety mounting. *Someone had gotten into their house.* The lives of both Kelly and his son had been threatened. He blew out an angry sigh. Kelly was going to listen to reason. This time he was not going to accept any damned excuses. If he had to play the role of bad guy, so be it. If pleas didn't work, maybe a bluff would. One way or the other, she was leaving that house.

He knew in time the press's feeding frenzy would die down. News of him having a child was enough of a story to bring the cameras to Texas. But no one wanted to read old news. Eventually, some new story would replace the old. The question was, how long until this was considered old? A call to Bret was necessary to ensure he didn't do anything to prolong this mess. The last thing any of them needed was for the manager to jump into the mayhem and milk it for all it was worth.

Putting his sunglasses in place, Jace got out of the truck with two members of his security team, one behind and one next to him. He ignored the shouts from the reporters and what had to be a quarter of the town's population standing behind the yellow tape. Three police cars, lights flashing, were blocking off the street, the officers trying unsuccessfully to disband the gawkers. With more calm than he felt, Jace opened the front door of the house and stepped inside.

Kelly was sitting on the couch, holding Henry. Matt sat on the floor next to her, reading letters. Tom, two of his men and two police officers stood in the small kitchen, quietly talking among themselves.

When Jace approached Kelly, she glared at him with a force that could hurt if it had any substance. But his concern effectively deflected any anger she might have and replaced it with some of his own. He crouched down next to the sofa, his face only inches from hers.

"Are you guys okay?"

"Physically. Obviously I don't appreciate that woman sneaking into my house and crawling up on my bed. You were supposed to do something. She broke my grandmother's vase."

"I'm about to do something. Kelly, this is finished. Do you understand?" His gaze caught hers and he didn't let go. "You're going to pack some clothes and you and Matt and Henry are moving to the ranch until this blows over."

"I don't want to live in your house."

"That's too damn bad." Jace could feel the tight control he had on his temper slipping. "You'd rather stay here and have someone break into your house again? Next time, it might be someone worse than that mentally disturbed woman. It might be the crazed idiot who wrote that letter. Don't be stupid, Kelly." He could hear the growl in his own voice.

Her quick intake of breath and the flash of surprise in her blue-green eyes told him he'd crossed the line. *Damn.* For the first time in his life, with Kelly of all people, the mother of his child, he was in danger of letting his anger override his common sense, doing exactly what he'd been afraid of for so many years. He clenched his jaw in an effort to maintain control. He had to keep it together. For Kelly. He felt a wave of guilt wash over him for what he'd said.

He reached out and gently took her face in his hands, determined to make her understand. "What if someone took

Henry?" Her eyes widened. Apparently the thought had not occurred to her. "A ransom demand is not that far-fetched."

"Then stop it," she snapped at him, a whispered plea. "You caused all of this. We were fine until you came back. Make them leave us alone."

"I'm trying, but it isn't that simple and you're smart enough to know that. I intend to do everything in my power to give the reporters what they want and see if I can make them leave. But the ranch is the only place I can protect you until that happens."

Jace let his hands drop and she looked down at Henry, who was sleeping peacefully in her arms. Jace could see the resentment in her face, the need for all of this to go away. She was frustrated and angry and probably a little scared all at the same time. He knew Kelly well enough to know she was going to try to bluff him out of their moving to the ranch. And no way was that going to happen.

"We can go to my friend Gerri's apartment and—"

"Do you really think that will make any difference?"

As she thought about his question, she moistened her lower lip with her tongue. He remembered all too well his mouth doing the same thing—tasting those lips, sucking the nectar from them before going deeper, enjoying the sweet taste he'd found in the hidden recesses of her mouth.

"I don't know. But I'm not moving to your house."

Jace ran a hand through his hair and huffed out some of the frustration. "Kelly, I can't legally make any demands of you, but Henry is my son and one way or the other, he is leaving this house. Now. It isn't safe. If I have to, I'll get a court order giving me temporary custody. And don't imagine any judge is going to stand by and let a five-month-old baby live in a threatening environment."

He hated playing the badass, but clearly they were in danger. If something happened to any of them he would never forgive himself. At this point it wasn't beneath him to toss her over his shoulder and carry her out kicking and screaming. If that's what it took, so be it. He *would* to keep them safe.

Pale and distraught, she looked up at him. Apparently just the mention of taking her child was enough to terrify her. Jace knew a surge of guilt for what he'd said, but he had to get her to relocate somewhere safe.

"Kelly? It doesn't have to be forever." He ignored the extra beat of his heart and the odd sinking feeling in his gut when he spoke those words.

She nodded. "You don't have to threaten."

"I apologize. You're making the right decision."

"Don't patronize me, either. You're giving me no choice. Of course I'm concerned for Henry's safety. You have to realize how…uncomfortable this will be for me. And in the meantime I expect you to make all this insanity go away."

She would try the patience of a saint. His eyes held hers for countless seconds, and he became aware that he was almost close enough to kiss her. He wanted to. Even now. Even in the middle of this crazy situation. He remembered holding her, making love to her. His body was hard with expectation and he knew she wouldn't be the only one uncomfortable while she lived under his roof. Only a few steps down the hall from his bedroom.

Kelly watched as Jace stood and walked over to Tom. There was a lot of nodding during their low, quiet discussion. Minutes later, they disappeared out the front door. Kelly listened to the muffled conversations as Jace apparently talked to the press. Ten minutes later, they came back inside.

"Here's what we're going to do," Jace said, returning to where Kelly sat. "It's almost dark. That will work to our advantage. Tom will have a car in front of the house in a few minutes, allowing time for some of the media to disperse. It's the same dark green SUV that's been taking you to work. Go to the car. Don't stop for anything. You know the drill."

Kelly stood and handed Henry to his father. Jace accepted the baby as if it were something he did every day. Which, come to think of it, he did. Or at least, he had for two weeks.

"I need to get some things together, unless you have his formula and plenty of diapers?" Knowing the answer, Kelly turned toward the bedroom. With her heart racing, she grabbed the baby bag and shoved it full of bottles, formula, baby food, clothes, diapers and a couple of stuffed toys. She pulled a small suitcase from the closet and packed jeans, assorted T-shirts, toiletries and a few more baby items.

Thirty minutes later it was time to go.

Matt stood waiting by the door. He wore a backpack, no doubt full of clothes, and held a tote bag with his books.

Jace stepped up behind them, still holding Henry. Kelly watched through the front windows as a green vehicle pulled up in front.

"It's here."

The short walk to the SUV was made without incident, although Kelly could feel the bevy of cameras recording every step. The throng of people standing behind the yellow tape surged forward when Jace emerged with his new baby. That provided a few seconds of apprehension but again, his security team took control. The ride to the grocery store parking lot where a helicopter awaited was made with no problems. Soon they were leaving the ground, quickly ascending into the darkened sky. Kelly watched the baby, afraid the sound would frighten him. But Henry took it in stride and continued to chew on Jace's shirt. Teething. Jace would have a major wet spot by the time they landed. Welcome to fatherhood.

"Cool," Matt muttered in fascination as he looked out the window.

In minutes they descended into the clearing of a pasture behind the stately home, setting down on a large round landing pad. The pilot immediately killed the engine, and they were escorted to waiting vehicles. The ride to the house was made in silence other than Henry's babble. Part of her wanted to be grateful to Jace for stepping in to keep Henry safe. The other part resented the fact that were it not for him, the protection wouldn't be needed in the first place.

The mansion was ablaze with lights. Jace escorted them down a path, his hand on her lower back.

"This is Carmen." Jace introduced a robust Hispanic woman who came forward with a welcoming smile as soon as they entered the house. "I need to speak with Tom. Carmen will take you all upstairs and show you where you'll be staying."

Not for long, Kelly thought, her mind slowly coming back on track. She took the baby from Jace and they followed the housekeeper up the stairs. Kelly remembered the day she'd cleaned the house and thought what a great place it was for a family. Never in a million years would she have guessed it would be her own family, let alone that she'd be living here with Jace. She swallowed hard.

The bedroom she was shown was only slightly smaller than the two rooms she'd cleaned a few weeks ago. The color scheme was green and blue pastel. It presented a relaxing and welcoming feel.

"You are next door, Mr. Matt," Carmen said in a strong accent. "This way. Make yourselves at home." She smiled at the baby in Kelly's arms. "I have four daughters, two sons and five grandbabies. Anything you need for your baby, you let me know, Mrs. Compton. I know what to do."

"Thank you. But I'm not…" Carmen and Matt disappeared around the corner before Kelly could explain she was *not* Mrs. Compton. She never would be. But why bother to correct her? They wouldn't be here long enough for it to make any difference.

Henry had finally wound down and was fast asleep in her arms. She put him in the center of the large bed, his little arms falling out to the side as he slept.

Living under Jace's roof was a bad idea. Every time Jace came close to her, memories jumped to the front of her mind. When he spoke, her eyes automatically focused on his mouth, on those lips that could do amazing things. When those all-knowing green eyes gleamed with passion, a chill went across her skin.

She had to keep this situation in perspective. There was no doubt any number of women who had felt exactly the same way about Jace Compton. She had to be one in a very long list who experienced the same pleasures in his arms. She was not a hormone-driven, nitwitted adolescent. She'd survived Jace once. She could do it again. She was here now only because of Henry. Even though the attraction was still strong, she would do well to remember the months after Jace had left and the fact that he'd never given her a second thought.

After unpacking, Kelly paced, not knowing what to do. She switched on the flat-screen TV and ran through the channel options, but found nothing that would hold her attention and turned it off. Her gaze fell on the door to the large bathroom. Venturing inside she passed through the powder room with its antique mirrors and vases of freshly cut flowers on dark marble countertops. Next was a shower large enough for four or five people and a whirlpool tub of equal size. She hurried back to the bedroom and placed pillows all around the edge of the bed to safeguard Henry while he slept. After covering the baby with his blue blanket and assuring herself he was sleeping peacefully, she headed back into the bathroom.

Pouring her favorite lavender bath salts into the quickly filling tub, she turned on the jets and climbed in. Lying back, she closed her eyes and gave in to the sheer luxury that enveloped her. The streams of the water coursing around her, against her back, her sides and neck, through her legs, soon began to reduce the stress of the past few days.

The memory of another time came unbidden to her mind.

There had been no tub at the ranch where Jace had stayed, but they'd made do with the shower.

For the first time in her life, Kelly saw a perfect example of the human male body. Broad shoulders blocked the water from reaching her as the moisture cascaded down over his corded neck and arms. Jace soaped his large hands and began to rub them slowly over every inch of her body, over her breasts, down her stomach, between her legs.

He was heavy with arousal and the air left her lungs as she stared, unable to tear her eyes away. She realized she'd never seen a man in this way before. There was no hiding under the blanket of modesty. He wanted to see every inch of her and offered her the same.

"See anything you like?"

Her gaze shot upward and met his. She could feel the blush spread over her face and neck. Obviously, Jace had no problem with modesty. He seemed totally unconcerned that she was seeing him naked. And aroused. Or that his size had her eyes bugging out of her head.

Jace had noted the blush. "Have you never seen a man before?" He tilted his head.

She swallowed. "Not...not like this."

He continued to watch her for several seconds. "How old were you? Late teens?"

"Yes."

"Quickie in the backseat?"

She nodded.

She saw a look of understanding cross his face. Instinct said her onetime experiment with teenage sex was not even close to what she was about to experience with the fully mature man who stood before her.

"Makes me curious what else you haven't experienced." His head dipped toward hers and he muttered against her lips, "Let's find out."

Without waiting for an answer, Jace took her lips in a deep, penetrating kiss that rocked her senses. He caught her hands and held them, palms up, as he poured the scented soap into them. Kelly stared at her hands for countless seconds, knowing what he was asking of her. Her heart beat in an accelerated rhythm as she contemplated what she was about to do.

Almost of their own accord, her hands moved to his large body. Slowly she began to rub the slick soap over his smooth skin, covering the hard wall of his chest and arms, loving the feel of the muscles that rippled beneath her hands.

She let them glide up to his massive shoulders and neck, then once again over his chest. She couldn't keep from looking into his eyes. He watched her with the look of a cat playing with a mouse. So intense was his focus, her hands stilled in their journey of discovery.

He took them and slowly pushed them down his body. "Touch me," he whispered, placing her fingers around his sex.

She tore her eyes from his face to look at the hard pound of flesh in her hands. Her gaze returned to his face, blue eyes meeting green, as she stood there, frozen, unable to release him yet unable to move. Her breathing becoming almost nonexistent.

"Let me help you, honey," he whispered. He began to move her hand against the silken flesh covering the underlying steel of his erection. It was an amazing sensation, and she caught on fast.

Jace lowered his head, and his lips again found hers. She opened her mouth and welcomed him in. His arms came around her as the warm water cascaded over their embrace.

His hand squeezed her hip then moved on to rub the sensitive area between her legs, encouraging her to open to him. She moved against his hand in an effort to quench the fire burning deep. Two fingers eased inside, and a shudder ran rampant through her entire body. With a muffled moan, she fell back against the shower wall as the mind-blowing sensations overtook her.

"Kelly," Jace groaned, his voice rough with need. Suddenly, his control seemed to snap. He lifted her, positioned her and pushed deep inside.

She felt a sudden draft of cold air mingle with the warm moisture of the bathroom seconds before his warm lips touched the sensitive curve where her neck and shoulder joined. A soft moan escaped her lips and, eyes closed, she turned into his mouth. Hungry lips covered hers, his tongue searching and finding what he sought. Her wet hands rose to hold his face, the need for him strong, essential. She gripped the back of his hair in a fist.

"Mmmm." He groaned, his deep, husky voice breaking the silence.

The memory ended with a shocking recoil, as if she'd had ice water thrown in her face. Her eyes shot open to find Jace leaning over the tub, his handsome face mere inches from hers. Kelly gasped in shock. She could feel herself flush with embarrassment over the memory she'd been reliving. Apparently, at some point they had merged with the present. She prayed his talents didn't include mind reading.

Jace's intense expression increased the simmering heat the daydream had generated. She held her arms over her breasts as she glared at Jace. He stood to full height, hands on his hips, his eyes moving over her naked body with an undeniable gleam.

"What are you doing in here?" Kelly spat the words, but Jace only pursed his lips as though hiding a grin and made no move to leave.

"I'm about to make love to you."

Seven

"You have no right to walk in here just because you own the house."

"You didn't appear to mind."

"I...I was just..."

He tilted his head, eyebrows raised, waiting for her to squirm out of this one. When she didn't reply, the gleam in those forest-green eyes intensified. "I know exactly what you were doing, Kelly. Instead of relying on memories, why don't you let me give you the real thing?"

Kelly frantically looked for a towel. "I need you to leave."

"Actually, I was headed to my room and heard Henry crying. After repeated knocks, I grew concerned. Would you rather I ignore his cries in the future?"

"He wasn't crying."

"As a matter of fact, he was. I gave him his pacifier and sat with him a few minutes and he went back to sleep."

"Well, you didn't have to come in *here*."

"I thought you might want to know about Henry." He pursed his lips, his green eyes glinting with humor. "There's nothing I haven't seen before, Kelly." His low voice caused shivers to run up her arms.

"That's not the point."

"No?"

"No."

He grabbed an oversize fluffy white towel and held it up for her. Kelly clambered out of the bath and down the few steps, and Jace wrapped the towel around her; his arms remained, holding her close.

"I've missed you." His low voice caused shivers to run over her skin.

"No, you haven't."

"Kelly, I want to work through this. I made mistakes. But they were not done intentionally."

She stepped back and his hands fell to his side.

"You miss the point. I don't care."

"I think you're letting your pride talk for you."

"And I think your libido is dictating to you."

"And that's a bad thing?"

She folded a corner of the towel between her breasts and moved away from him into the dressing area. She refused to argue. Especially when she might not win. Grabbing her comb, she began to work through the tangles, praying he would leave.

He stood in the entrance to the bathroom, leaning casually against the wall, watching her. The mirrored reflection did nothing to diminish his pure male presence, making her want to do all sorts of things she shouldn't. Unbidden, her mind kept reliving moments from before, and Jace was apparently more than willing to repeat every single one of them. She wouldn't go there again. She couldn't. The first time, his leaving, his lying, had almost destroyed her. For her own sake, and Henry's, she would not jump back in that rabbit hole again.

Having finished her task, she returned to the bedroom in search of fresh clothes. A peek toward the bed confirmed Henry was fast asleep, his blue pacifier moving slightly as he sucked on it. Jace stood next to her gazing down at the baby, and then shifted his focus to her. What she saw in his eyes was pride for his son, but more: she saw concern. He honestly cared about his son. He'd heard Henry crying and stopped to check on him. The blue pacifier was proof Jace had been telling the truth. That meant he'd sat next to the baby and given comfort until Henry went back to sleep. For perhaps the first time since they'd met, she saw more than a sexy body and killer smile. She saw a glimpse into the heart of the person Jace was inside. And that was a little bit daunting. She didn't want to like Jace Compton.

"I need to check on Matt." She walked to the bureau, removing a clean shirt and jeans.

Jace nodded, this time taking the hint, and walked out the door.

Matt was happily absorbed in a car racing game on his Xbox. To him, this was a grand adventure. He'd better enjoy it while it lasted.

She returned to her room and pulled on her old cotton gown and slipped into bed next to Henry. She had to leave here. She couldn't stay in this house with Jace. He might want to pick up where they'd left off, and she knew her defenses were sadly lacking. Loving him might not be something she could control. Making love to him was not going to happen.

Regardless of how much she might want it to.

"But I don't understand." Kelly blinked back the tears. "I had a week of vacation and it's only been…five days." *Crap.* She'd just quashed her own defense.

"Are you saying you'll be back on Monday?" Her boss was usually a fair man, but this was a low blow. "I should warn you, the press are still camped out at all the exits here. Frankly, this is becoming a problem."

The voice on the other end of the line was apologetic but firm. The work was piling up and they had to get someone in to deal with it.

The call ended and Kelly sank down onto one of the kitchen chairs, totally devastated. Reluctantly, she'd agreed to give up her job. Her boss had called her work top-notch and said that if there was an opening when she was ready to come back, she would certainly be considered for reemployment. He'd again offered his apologies, and then it was over. The call as well as her hope for the immediate future.

This was a nightmare that kept on giving.

"Hey, Kelly." Matt hurried into the den. "Turn on the TV." Matt found the remote and switched on the set himself. A news conference was in full swing. "Now we know where Jace has been for two days."

"I didn't know we cared."

"Yes, I've always liked Texas." Jace's handsome face filled the screen as he spoke.

"Rumors are rampant that you and a woman, Kelly Michaels, have a child? Can you comment on that?" a reporter asked off camera.

Without hesitation, Jace nodded, that award-winning grin flashing perfect white teeth. "Yes. We have a son. We're both very happy. Very excited."

A bevy of questions followed his statement. Kelly didn't see how he could understand any of them, but he soon responded, "I'll provide some pictures when he's older. I'm sure you can appreciate the safety concerns."

Another round of questions, and then, "I can't say where we will live at this juncture. Currently we are enjoying some solitude in Texas. There's always a chance we'll come back to LA. We haven't made a decision."

"Are you planning to get married?" someone asked.

Kelly's heart stopped in her throat, anticipating what Jace would say to that.

"Right now we haven't made any plans. We just want to enjoy our son and some quiet time together. I hope you can respect our privacy, give us a little room."

The subject changed to his next film role. Did Jace think he would get the lead in the rumored blockbuster due to start filming in three months? Again that smile. "You guys will probably know that before I do." He got the laughing response he no doubt intended. After a few more softballs like that, he called an end to the press conference. "Okay. That's all I have for today. Thanks."

He turned and disappeared into the hotel lobby, security stepping in to prevent the throngs of reporters from following him inside. At least he was keeping his promise to do what he could to make the media leave them alone. She just hoped it worked.

"Awesome." Matt turned off the television. "Tell me you're not excited to be here."

"I'm not excited to be here." Kelly met her brother's eyes with a deadpan expression.

"Kelly—"

"I just lost my job, Matt. Soon we'll have no home to go back to. And before you say it, no. We can't continue to live here." She wasn't about to go into the reasons with her kid brother. How could she even begin to explain the complicated emotional mess between Jace and herself? And where would she find another job? In the small community, jobs weren't plentiful.

"I need a personal assistant."

Kelly swung around to find a petite woman with beautiful auburn hair standing in the open doorway. The intricate lines around her eyes seemed to make them sparkle. Her welcoming smile looked very familiar.

"I'm Mona," she introduced herself. "Jason's mother. And you must be Kelly."

"Yes."

"I'm sorry I wasn't here to greet you when you arrived," she said as she walked toward them. "It took longer than anticipated to take care of some lose ends before leaving California. This must be Matt? Very nice to meet you. Jason has talked nonstop about you both."

She stopped in front of where Kelly sat balancing Henry on her knees. "And who is this handsome little man?" The look that softened her face spoke volumes.

"This is Henry." Kelly looked up and smiled.

A wet sheen glistened in the older woman's eyes. For the longest time, Mona stared, unmoving, at the baby in Kelly's arms, her gaze taking in every inch of her grandson, from his head to his feet. Kelly held him with his back against her chest. He kicked his feet while he tried his best to fit his little fist into his mouth. Jace's mother tried valiantly to hold back the tears of joy. It was all there in her face: overwhelming delight, pride and immediate acceptance.

"Would you care to hold him?" Henry loved people. He'd never been intimidated or shown any fear of strangers, and this was someone he might want to know better. Mona pulled out a chair and sat down. She took a moment to compose herself, wiping away the tears now falling from her face. Then she smiled at Kelly.

"I would love to."

Matt headed for his room and another round on Xbox. Mona took Henry in her arms and for a time seemed to be mesmerized. Kelly sat down, content to watch the first meeting between Henry and his grandmother unfold.

As it turned out, she was serious about the job offer. Mona headed an organization that raised money for several charities. One in particular that helped abused women and children was apparently very special to her. For that one she always held an annual ball and banquet in early October. And she needed assistance.

Kelly wasn't entirely sure how Mona did it, but Kelly soon found herself agreeing to help and worse, agreeing to continue to help until the charity ball, which was over a month away. She was losing it. That's all there was to it. But she would not live under Jace's roof forever. Absolutely not. She might be crazy but she wasn't stupid.

She'd give the big news event another week to blow over. Then no matter what, she was taking Matt and Henry and going home. Remaining in Jace's house was a seriously foolish idea. She liked to think she was strong as far as determination and resolve. But she knew if she had a weak spot,

Jace was it. If she caved, she'd be setting herself up for more heartache. That was something she didn't want or need.

As the helicopter began its descent, Jace again thought about who would be waiting for him at the door when he arrived. Kelly. His son. Matt and his mom. A small family. The kind of family he'd wished for most of his life. Granted, he wasn't exactly returning to a loving family unit who would welcome him with open arms, but he wasn't coming back to an empty house. It was a family. Sort of. And it was his.

Matt already had become a great friend. And Henry…a living miracle. Something Jace had never let himself envision. His son. A little face that would someday resemble his own. A young life with everything ahead of him. And Jace wanted to give him the world.

Kelly was the core. She brought it all together. She was the reason he was here, the driving force that had prompted him to purchase this ranch in Texas. The time spent with her last year had been nothing short of bliss. This community of kind strangers, along with the gently sloping hills and valleys, had brought serenity to his soul. It was the dream of a future he'd never before let himself imagine, but for a brief moment in time, he could pretend. Had it all been his imagination? He intended to find out.

He sighed and pulled a hand over his face. The only thing worse than wanting a real home and family was having one and knowing it couldn't last.

"Where is Kelly?" Jace asked his mother as he entered the large kitchen. His mom sat at the table munching on a slice of Carmen's homemade butternut bread. She didn't answer his question, merely took another sip of her coffee, not meeting his eyes. Jace frowned, his senses going on full alert.

"Mom?"

"I believe she had some things she needed to do."

"Did she leave the ranch?"

"Don't worry, dear. She'll be back as soon as she can."

Dammit to hell. He took the cell from his pocket and punched Tom's number. His head of security answered on the first ring.

"She said she had to get some things and she wanted her car," Tom said, answering Jace's unasked question. "Murphy drove her to town, and when they reached her house she told him to leave. Jace, you know we're limited in what we can do. If she tells us to get lost…"

"Yeah, I know. Was there anyone at her house?"

"Just a few dozen determined gawkers. She'll be fine if she stays under the radar. I don't foresee any problems."

Obviously Tom didn't know Kelly.

"What time did she leave?"

"Ten o'clock."

"Thanks."

Kelly was independent as hell. He just hadn't thought she would push her luck to this extent. She knew what could happen. Apparently, whatever she was up to, in her mind it was worth taking the risk.

Jace glanced at his watch and frowned. Two o'clock. It didn't take half a day to make the drive from town. Jace headed outside and jumped into the truck. Three miles down the road, he spotted her, trudging toward his place, baby in her arms, her ponytail swinging side to side.

"Do I need to guess?" he asked as he pulled up next to her.

She didn't look amused.

He threw the truck into Park and walked around to open the passenger door, helping her and the baby inside, and then tossed the bags, purse and brown paper sack she was carrying onto the backseat. He hoped to hell that wasn't her lunch, but he suspected it was. Miss Independence. He had to wonder how far she'd walked.

He turned the pickup around and headed back to the ranch. "I'm getting you a phone."

"I have a phone. I can't get a signal out here."

"Then I'm getting you a better one."

"No, you're not. The one I have works fine in town."

"What about while you're living out here? It's not smart to have a baby and no way to call for help if you need it."

"You're right. I'll buy a new one eventually."

"And what are you going to do between now and then if something happens?"

"With no transportation, I doubt it will be a problem," she answered dully. "First, I need to get the car fixed."

"That piece of junk isn't worth repairing," Jace muttered under his breath. He glanced her way. She was smiling down at the baby, who cooed and held on to his mother's finger. "Pick out a new car and have it delivered tomorrow."

"No."

Jace gritted his teeth and rubbed his neck. "You have got to be the most stubborn, hardheaded woman I've ever come across in my life."

"*Me?* Look in the mirror. Why do you keep pushing? Why do you keep insisting I take things from you? Frankly, it's getting old."

Goddammit.

"I don't need your help. We've already had this discussion. Maybe you should write it down and tape it to your forehead?"

Kelly was the only woman who came close to bringing him to his knees out of pure frustration. And she didn't have to touch him to do it.

"Why did you go into town?"

"I wanted my car."

He snorted.

She glared.

"You mother kindly offered me a job. Temporarily. I have to have transportation to get to the ranch."

"You're staying at the ranch."

"We can't keep living in your house."

"Why not?"

She presented him with a deadpan stare. The silence was deafening.

Okay, so he knew why not. The attraction between them, the pheromones, so powerful that they pulled him to her like a winch and a steel cable. He would have to be dead not to feel it. But he didn't want her to leave the ranch, and it wasn't only because of the safety issue. And it wasn't solely because he wanted to take her to his bed.

He wanted Kelly to like him again.

"Maybe there's another option."

"Like what?" She frowned.

Jace applied the brakes. Coming to a halt, he threw the truck into Reverse. Backing up some fifty feet he turned into a small, one-lane gravel road that disappeared into the trees. In less than a quarter of a mile the road ended at a small white house. Jace pulled up to the side and killed the motor.

"When I bought the ranch, there were four small houses on the property, originally built for ranch hands. I had them updated along with the main house. The ranch foreman lives in one, my head trainer in the second. The third was redesigned for my security team. This is the fourth. It's empty. It has its own entrance separate from the ranch, three bedrooms, a bath and a small kitchen."

"Are you saying…? I can't move here."

"Why not? The house is just sitting here. I have no plans to use it."

She had to admit it was better than living in his house. Barely. Kelly had been concerned about his close proximity if she worked for his mother. Living in his house was her single biggest worry when she'd agreed to help Mona. But this might be a temporary solution.

Or not.

"I don't know…"

"Kelly, don't be so stubborn about everything. This is a great idea."

She snorted at the absurdity. "No, it's not."

She didn't like it. A sense of unease churned inside. If she moved here, she would be totally reliant on Jace for everything. And it didn't come with an expiration date. There was no until-the-end-of-the-month move-out date. And that wasn't a good feeling.

"At least think about it. It makes sense."

"I like living in town."

"You haven't seen the inside of the cabin."

"I don't care. Why would I move out here just for a few months? Seems like an awful lot of trouble. I'm already indebted to your mother for a job. I'm not going to ask you for a place to live as well."

"I don't recall you asking."

Kelly turned to face him. His vivid emerald eyes made her want to waver, but she held firm. "Jace, I have two people who rely on me. I can't take the chance you won't suddenly decide to sell this place. Then where would we be? No job. No home. And you'd be gone without so much as a backward glance, just like before."

A glint of resentment darkened his eyes to the color of singed leaves; the barely perceptible narrowing of his eyes said he was ready to defend himself against her challenge. His jaw muscles tightened, his mouth straightening to a hard line. Then in an instant it was gone, replaced with a look more closely resembling determination.

"You will *never* have to worry about a job or a place to live or money in your bank account. *Deal with it.*"

Her eyes narrowed. "You might be okay with your ex-lover living on your ranch like some kind of leech. I'm not. I'm sure I've already been branded a gold digger. I *hate* that. Moving here… Word would get out and only make it worse."

"I really don't give a damn what anyone else thinks," Jace responded, slight traces of annoyance in his tone. He looked at her, his olive eyes intense and thoughtful. Then he dropped a bombshell. "But if you're that concerned about public opinion, marry me, Kelly. Problem solved."

Eight

Kelly had to steady herself. "That isn't funny."

"I didn't intend it to be."

"Then you're out of your mind."

"Why?"

She turned away from him, looking out the side window without really seeing. She shook her head, swallowing down the bile that rose in her throat. "Do you honestly expect me to respond to a joke? Having a child together does not a marriage make."

"I can come up with more reasons."

"Being good together in bed is not a valid reason, either." It didn't take the mental aptitude of Einstein to guess where his mind was going.

"At least you admit it." He raised his eyebrows as if daring her to deny it.

Kelly fought to keep him from seeing the hurt churning inside. She'd never expected him to say those words even in jest. A little part of her died at the realization that Jace viewed marriage as a joke. A prank. To him life was a game. That fact above all made his words seem almost cruel.

This was a pie-in-the-face wake-up call about how Jace viewed life. She'd always suspected, but never really let herself believe it.

She'd had a front-row seat during her parents' marital atrocity. She'd seen her father's feelings of obligation turn to disinterest, then disgust and finally hatred. He'd maliciously mocked her mother's love, seemingly taking glee in her anguish.

Her mother may have settled for a man who didn't love her, but Kelly was not interested in starring in the sequel. She wanted someone who loved her and wanted to be with her, not a man who felt trapped by circumstance. Despite the deterioration of her parents' marriage, Kelly still believed in the rightness of marriage. It was an ideal she held close to her heart, harboring a childhood dream that maybe someday she could have a chance to do it better. But it wouldn't be with Jace Compton, Mr. Love-'em-and-Leave-'em.

There was a time she would have jumped at the chance to marry the man she'd met and fallen in love with fifteen months ago. But even then, it had to be because he loved her. Not because he felt obligated.

The only reason Jace was spending time with her now was because of his son and the mess he'd created in their lives. Once his baby revelation died down, he'd be out of here so fast his exit would suck the leaves off the trees. Marry today. Divorce tomorrow. Fodder for the gossips and a publicity boon. No harm done. Life goes on.

How had his life morphed into such a bizarre existence?

She blinked the moisture from her eyes and gritted her teeth to overcome her momentary weakness. Inside, a mature, sensible woman battled an immature fool who was willing to believe anything, go anywhere, do anything, just to be with him. Reach for the stars and the delusion of happily-ever-after.

The single common thread between the two conflicting forces was love. She loved Jace. Behind all the barriers protecting her heart, she'd never stopped. But he must never know. She couldn't bear the shame and the mockery that would undoubtedly follow if Jace and the world ever found out.

"Come on. At least look at the cabin."

"No." Her voice was almost a whisper. She released her death grip on the seat, folding her hands in her lap.

"I would prefer you stay in the main house but I understand your need for some privacy. At least wait until you've seen the house before you decide?"

"Jace…"

Walking around the front of the F250, he opened the passenger-side door.

"Come on. Get out."

"Please. Just let it go."

The humor left his face. It was as though he'd suddenly realized something had changed. He looked at her questioningly.

"I respect your need for independence, Kelly. But you're letting your hatred of me overshadow your common sense. I have no intention of selling this place. Mom needs it as much as I do." His eyes were steady as his gaze held hers. "And we both need you."

His deep voice and those last words shook her to the core. Kelly wanted to reach out and touch the strong, handsome face only inches from her own. She wanted to feel his arms around her again despite how badly he'd hurt her. But she'd already used up her share of idiocy for a lifetime.

"I don't hate you, Jace."

For long seconds, neither moved. Then Jace leaned toward her. Ignoring the warning bells going off inside her head, Kelly didn't back away. His lips touched hers, warm, tentative, as though asking for permission. The subtle fragrance of his natural male scent surrounded her. She felt the slight rasp of his day-old five-o'clock shadow as his tongue entered her mouth, bringing with it the rich taste of coffee and the tantalizing taste of pure male. Her right hand lifted to rest on his powerful shoulder. God help her. It was as if fifteen long months had shriveled down to yesterday, his touch both familiar and new.

With a sudden squeal and a string of happy jabber from

Henry, who chose that moment to awaken from the nap in Kelly's arms, Jace drew back, watching her closely. Frowning, he lifted her face to his, his thumbs gently wiping away her tears.

"Why the tears, Kelly?"

She gave her best impression of a laugh. "Don't know what you're talking about."

He continued to watch her, his look intense. "Kelly—?"

"Just don't say anything else, okay? I'm...I'm just grateful. For the offer of the house. That's all."

She knew that look on his face. He didn't buy the gratitude excuse for a second. Unlike him, she was no actress. He would let it go for now, but he wouldn't drop it completely.

He reached to take Henry from her arms, and then held out his hand to her. Kelly reluctantly accepted his help getting out of the truck. His hand was big and warm, his grip strong and sure around hers. The baby laughed, then began sucking on his forefinger, his feet in a simulated run. They walked to the front of the cabin where Jace unlocked the door.

It was nice. The small kitchen was the same size as the one in her rental. A breakfast bar separated it from the living area, and a high-beamed ceiling gave a spacious feel.

"The bedrooms and bathroom are through there." Jace nodded in a direction behind her. The entire house was fresh and clean. The bathroom fixtures and kitchen appliances appeared new. It was already furnished with a sofa, stools for the breakfast bar and beds.

Jace dangled a key in front of her.

"It isn't bait. This is not a trap. It's yours if you want it. No expectations. No hidden agenda. As you saw, it has its own entrance, its own driveway. You'll have the only key." He tilted his head and waited for her decision.

Chewing her bottom lip, she looked back over the spacious room and then returned her gaze to Jace. "Why are you doing this?"

"Does there have to be a reason other than practicality?" He readjusted his stance as though ready for another battle.

"That doesn't answer my question, does it?"

Her mind said she was about to make another huge mistake. She hated weakness, especially in herself. Being weak caused regrets and all kinds of pain. Why did everything have to be so hard? Why did her world suddenly seem to revolve around this man? It was like being strapped to a merry-go-round as it spun faster and faster out of control until the very breath was sucked from your lungs. By the time you realized you had to get off, you knew doing so was really going to hurt.

"You have to live somewhere, and staying at your house in town right now is not a good option. You don't want to live in the main house with me. This is a sensible, workable alternative. The rent on your house in town has already been paid through the end of the year—so don't feel you're trapped here. And I intend to replace your car—which I refuse to argue about."

Despite what had just happened between them, Kelly reached out and took the key from his hand. Her heartbeat increased as she turned it over and over in her fingers. She nodded her head in reluctant acceptance. It was only a couple of hundred yards farther away from him than she was now. But she'd take what she could get.

Jace stepped outside, still holding Henry. "This path leads to the back door of the house. Follow it in the opposite direction and you'll be at the main barn."

Together they returned to his truck. He helped her inside, handed her the baby and got behind the wheel.

"You had no right to pay my rent."

Jace didn't comment as he started the motor but just pursed his lips, obviously biting back a grin, and shook his head as though he'd expected her to say exactly that. She didn't like charity and she damn sure didn't like being a foregone conclusion.

They headed back to the main road, made the short ride around to Jace's front gate and on to his house in silence. Kelly had to wonder where all this would end. She was increasingly becoming part of his life and it frightened her. Putting up a brave front was hard to do. And getting more difficult every day. A wave of reality washed over her and she swallowed hard. Change was always a scary thing. In her life it had never been for the better.

It's only temporary, she reminded herself. *It isn't forever.*

On Friday afternoon, three of Jace's ranch hands moved the boxes she'd packed from her house in town to the cabin on the ranch. Jace stood next to her while they unloaded the truck. He appeared content to hold Henry, even responded to his gibberish. It surprised Kelly how Jace and the baby seemed to have already formed a bond. While it worried her, she had to resign herself to the fact that it was done. If Henry became upset when it was time for them to leave here, she'd have to handle it then as best she could. Mr. Playboy of the Year was definitely becoming a hands-on father. Who would have thought?

"That's the last of it," the ranch foreman told Kelly as two lanky cowboys walked out of the cabin. "We put the baby bed together for you. Looks like all that's left is for you to unpack and settle in."

"Thanks so much, Sam. Thanks, guys."

"I appreciate it, Sam," Jace added, ambling up to where they stood.

"You bet. Jace, you take care of that baby." Sam grinned and seated himself behind the wheel of the old truck. The cowboys tipped their hats, already walking toward the barn. "Good to have you here at the ranch, Mrs. Compton." Sam gunned the motor and with a wave out the window, took off down the driveway.

"I'm not... Ahhh." Kelly stomped her foot in frustration. "*Why* does everyone keep calling me that?"

Jace's free hand shot up, palm toward her. "I'm not saying a word."

With a glare in his direction, Kelly took Henry and went into the house. Standing in the center of the living room, she glanced at the boxes stacked around her. It seemed so... permanent. The anxiety she'd been pushing aside all week came back front and center. She couldn't let go of the feeling that this was a bad decision.

She put Henry in his swing and began unpacking and arranging their things. Several hours later everything was done, the beds were made, the empty boxes flattened and placed outside next to the small front porch.

That evening after she fed and bathed Henry and put him to bed for the night, she ventured outside. Two old metal chairs, one yellow, one green, sat on the extended concrete slab that served as a front porch. The weather was unusually cool for this time of year. Slipping into the nearest chair, she leaned back, closed her eyes and savored the beautiful evening.

"Looks like someone is enjoying this fine weather."

Kelly jumped at the sound of the male voice.

"Sorry." The man held his hands up. "Didn't mean to scare you."

"That's okay." Her eyes focused on the tall, lean man standing a few feet in front of her. His shaggy blond hair and welcoming smile immediately put her at ease. "It seemed like a good time to put my feet up and relax."

"I know the feeling." He took off his hat. "I'm Sylvester Decker, one of the trainers here at the ranch. People just call me Decker."

"Oh. Of course. It's nice to meet you. Occasionally I see you guys leading a horse from one area to another. There's a chestnut, almost the color of a new penny, with flaxen mane and tail and three white socks. Beautiful."

"That would be Classy Lady." He put one foot on the concrete slab and leaned toward her, resting his arms on his knee and holding his hat in his hands. "And you're right. She's a nice filly. Great bloodlines, but in the racing game, that's not an absolute guarantee. You should come to the main barn area sometime and see them up close. Do you ride?"

"I used to. One of my best friends lives at the neighboring ranch, the Bar H. When we were in school, she used to invite me out for weekends and we would go riding. It was great."

Decker suddenly straightened and took a step back. "Hey, Jace."

"Decker," Jace responded as he stepped out of the shadows into the muted light from the barn. Jace had obviously followed the path from the house, but neither Kelly nor Decker had heard him approach until he was standing in front of her small cabin.

"I just stopped by to welcome our new neighbor to the ranch."

Jace didn't reply. He watched the man like a predator protecting his territory. His eyes almost glowed in the darkness, giving the impression of a panther returning to its lair to find another male stalking the entrance. The air suddenly became thick with the sizzle of animosity. Kelly couldn't help but wonder if Decker sensed it or if it was just her imagination.

"Well, I'll leave you two to talk. It was nice to meet you, Kelly."

"You, too, Decker."

"Don't forget to come see the fillies."

"Thanks. I'd like that."

The cowboy slipped his hat back in place, his long strides carrying him down the path toward the barn until he disappeared into the night.

Jace motioned to the chair next to Kelly. "Mind if I sit down?" He didn't wait for an answer. He lowered his bulk into the old metal rocker, leaned back and brought one booted foot to rest on his knee. "So how goes it with you and Mom? Everything okay?"

"She's great. I love the work. I was afraid it was... That she offered me the job because..."

"You thought it was charity."

"Yeah." Kelly nodded. "But it's not. There's really a lot to do."

"Mom had two full-time assistants when she lived in Los Angeles." Jace cut her a glance, a smile tugging at the corners of his lips. "Be careful what you asked for."

Kelly had to smile. "We're finishing the invitations and considering a theme for the charity ball in October."

"Ah, yes. Mom usually hosts several events a year for different causes, but this one is her favorite. Over the years, it has taken on a life of its own. Be forewarned."

The soft glow of the lights from the barn in the distance provided the only light. Somewhere deep in the trees, a lone cricket chirped and two owls called to each other. Suddenly the tiny porch seemed very intimate. With only a soft breeze passing through the trees, Jace's heady male scent seemed to surround her. She could feel his heat. Her body automatically gravitated toward him. She couldn't help but wonder if he knew the effect he had on her. But no doubt he had the same effect on most women. It was as natural to him as breathing, and he'd probably stopped paying any attention years ago.

He adjusted his position and his knee touched her leg. The small point of contact became a focal point in her mind. She swallowed convulsively. This close, he was entirely too disturbing. Kelly hadn't realized the chairs were so close. Now she fought the temptation to move hers. But her mind and body were giving mixed signals on which way to move it. Jace didn't seem to notice the contact. He sat back, appearing completely relaxed.

"It's too bad there are so many trees out here," Jace said. "They block the view of the sky."

Her gaze automatically veered upward. All she could see were the leaves on the lower branches, which caught the glow of light from the barn.

"I remember watching Texas sunsets until they faded into night. Suddenly, the sky became full of stars." She felt his eyes on her. "Everywhere."

"Yes," she whispered before she could catch herself. She knew he was referring to the nights they'd spent together, him holding her close while they watched the stars through the window twinkle in the midnight sky. Then Jace would put his lips on hers and make similar stars burst in an explosive grand finale before the free fall back to earth.

"Do you still look at the stars, Kelly?"

That brought her out of the past and slammed her face-first into the present.

"No." She shook her head. "Not anymore." She cleared her throat. "Decker said you have some good bloodlines."

"I like what I see so far."

Kelly chanced a glance in his direction. He was looking directly at her; a wicked light glittered in his eyes. She quickly looked away. "I grew up with the cattle ranches, but never saw anything like you're putting together."

He nodded. "It's a challenge. A lot more involved than I originally thought, and we're just getting started. Every day is a new challenge. It's not easy, but definitely well worth the effort. I'm hoping patience and determination will pay off in the long run."

Kelly swallowed hard. She could swear every word out of his mouth referred to her. To them.

"Kelly..." he said, his voice husky.

She couldn't stop herself from turning toward him. Their gazes met and held. In that instant, she wanted to again feel his lips on hers. She wanted to turn the page and let them start fresh. Allow her the chance to make this superstar believe in love. The forever kind. The kind that wasn't a joke. Unbidden, her gaze lowered to his mouth, so tempting. So close.

Electricity sizzled in the air. Her heartbeat increased as the heat of unwanted arousal bloomed in her lower regions, causing her body temperature to rise. He leaned toward her.

He gripped the back of her neck and gently drew her to him. His tongue moistened her lips, tempting her to open to him. She drew air deep into her lungs, but rather than clearing her head and pulling her out of the spell she seemed to be under, inhaling his essence tempted her to come closer. With a fevered sigh, she tilted her head the slightest bit and opened her lips, and Jace took full advantage, entering her mouth, deepening the embrace.

A filament of sanity threaded its way into her mind, and she clung to that small thread. With all the internal strength she could muster, she turned her head, separating her lips from the smoldering heat of his.

"I should go and check on Henry," she whispered, still fighting to retain some clarity of thought, her voice breathy from his kiss. Jace's gaze held hers for a long moment before he released her. Taking a deep breath, Kelly pushed against the metal arms of the chair and rose to her feet. More than anything, she wanted to kiss him forever. She wanted to relive the passion that detonated the stars. And she was edging ever closer to doing something really stupid. "If you'll excuse me, I'll say good-night."

The gleam in his dark eyes clearly told her he understood more than she wanted him to. "Good night, Kelly."

She hurried inside and closed the door. When she was sure Jace was gone, she stepped back outside and crossed the lawn until she came to a spot where the trees parted and offered an unobstructed view of the sky.

She'd lied to Jace. She'd never stopped looking at the stars. At *their* star. One winked at her and she smiled, peace settling in her heart for the first time in a long while.

Kelly had wondered if he remembered the dinners across

a candlelit table, the days spent together under the warm rays of the sun, the nights in his arms as they watched the night sky. She'd doubted it. Compared to the beautiful women he dated, she was nothing. A piece of wheat toast compared to a fine French pastry.

But she'd been wrong. Jace remembered.

But all things considered, did it really make any difference?

Nine

There was something going on with Kelly. It was barely perceptible, and if it were not for his years of training as an actor, he wouldn't have picked up on it. But there was something infinitesimally different in her voice, in her eyes. She had distanced herself from him, even more so than when he'd first come back to Calico Springs. She'd erected a wall that hadn't been there before. He just couldn't get a handle on what had happened. What had changed?

As he walked back to the house, his mind whirled in quiet speculation. He'd noticed the difference around the time she agreed to move into the cabin. Had moving from the main house upset her? Did she want to stay with him instead? Surely she knew the choice was hers. He replayed their conversation in his mind. He recalled that her only objection had involved wanting to return to her home.

She seemed to like her job. His mother had told him Kelly was a delight to work with. Her attention to detail, her intuitiveness as to the direction his mom wanted to go with the charity event, her suggestions... Everything was great. His mother had a baby bed, a swing and a truckload of toys brought in and they were both enjoying Henry.

But something was off. He had no doubt it was something he'd said or done, but he had no clue what it could be.

Whatever the reason, Kelly was right. He should keep his distance. He needed to stop pursuing her. He couldn't give her the forever she undoubtedly wanted and deserved. And Henry. He knew he needed to stay clear of the baby.

But he was drawn to him just like he was to Kelly. It was crazy. Something inside compelled him to be as close to them as possible while it lasted. Henry had already grown so much during their short stay on the ranch. By the time Jace returned from another film project, his son would be walking. And talking. And if Jace distanced himself the way he needed to, the coming years would pass without him ever knowing his son. Without Henry knowing his father.

All things considered, maybe that wasn't such a bad thing.

Kelly straightened the desk and gathered Henry's things in preparation to leave for the day. Before she could pick up Henry, Jace stepped inside the room.

"Can I borrow your assistant?" He looked first at his mom before switching his gaze to Kelly. "Thought you might like to see the horses. I remember you mentioning it to Decker."

Kelly glanced at Mona and received a nod of encouragement. "Henry will be just fine. And I don't mind a bit. You go ahead."

Jace's hand was warm against her lower back as he guided her down the path to the large structure. It was wrong to enjoy his closeness, his touch. But she did. And she was not about to ask him to stop. When they reached the wide-open double doors of the barn they were greeted with knickers from the stalls on both sides of the aisle. The earthy scent of rich, sweet alfalfa, leather and the horses filled the air. The beautiful chestnut filly she'd seen being led back to the barn one day immediately caught her eye through the bars on the top half of the stalls. As Kelly approached, the filly's ears pricked forward in curiosity as she continued chewing her evening grain.

"She's so beautiful," Kelly murmured. The young mare's coat gleamed like polished copper. "I saw her being led from the round exercise pen once. She's even more magnificent up close."

Jace smiled, reached forward and opened the top half of the stall door, giving Kelly unrestricted access. The filly stepped over and put her head through the opening. Kelly couldn't resist stroking the silky neck.

"Hey, sweetheart." She couldn't contain the full grin from spreading across her face. "Oh Jace, she's amazing."

"Most thoroughbreds are pretty high-strung. This one seems a lot calmer. Don't know how that will play out on the track. But she seems to genuinely like people."

"Does she like carrots? Or apples?"

"I really couldn't tell you." He appeared surprised at the question.

"I'll bet she does. And she'll be fast, won't you, pretty lady? I never knew you liked horses, Jace."

He stepped around to the other side of the filly, giving her a pat. "As a kid, I dreamed about someday having a ranch." He shrugged. "There used to be a small carnival that came to our area once or twice a year and it had pony rides for the kids. That's the first place I headed. Never wanted to get down. Then a few years ago, I had to learn to ride pretty proficiently for a part in a film. Once I was trained, every spare second I wasn't needed on the set, I would spend riding. We were filming in New Mexico on a large ranch near Santa Fe. You could ride for miles."

"I can relate. Your neighbor just down the road at the Bar H is one of my oldest friends. Growing up we spent most of our summers on the back of a horse. We'd pack food and water in the saddlebags and off we'd go. Her dad used to get so mad when we were late getting back. A few times it was well past dark and he was *livid*." Kelly grinned at the memories. "Their land backed up to the national forest and grasslands. We found an old gate and that was it. We headed for that entrance every time."

Kelly glanced from the filly to Jace. He was grinning, the

small laugh lines showing at the corners of his eyes while attractive grooves appeared on either side of his mouth. "What?"

He shook his head. "I just never pictured you for a cowgirl."

"I don't know if that's a compliment or an insult." She smiled up at him. "But I love horses. I think your place might border the grasslands, as well. You might want to have someone check it out. You can ride for days. Shea and I would get so turned around. Oh my gosh. I still don't know how we always managed to make it home. I think the horses were our saving grace."

She saw an amused glitter in his dark eyes. She swallowed nervously, not believing she'd just talked so freely with him. But then, she always had. Between them, conversation had flowed easily as they discovered more and more about each other, their likes and dislikes. They had so many common interests. Food. Music. Gazing at the stars on cloudless nights.

"I did the same thing," he said, closing the stall door. "I would ride out so far from base camp in New Mexico, at times I had no idea which way was up. But the horse always knew where its evening meal would be."

In this environment with the scents and sounds of nature surrounding them, and the easy banter between them, Jace was again the guy she met almost a year and a half ago. Silent alarms began clanging in her head. Needing to put some distance between them, she walked down to the next stall. Inside was a horse with a slightly darker coat than the filly.

"This is Chesapeake Dream," Jace offered as he opened the top of the door.

Like the first filly, she came forward and curiously sniffed the two humans who stood in front of her. "She's the one we think will bring it home. She's not yet three, so Lee is taking her training slow, but she's been on the track a couple of times and has really shown some speed."

Kelly reached out to run her hand down the velvety neck. After a few minutes, Jace closed the stall door and Kelly moved down the aisle. She passed an empty stall and proceeded to the next one. Through the metal bars, she saw a magnificent thoroughbred with a coat as black as polished ebony. This one was a lot bigger than the others.

She opened the top of the stall door as Jace had previously done, but this time the greeting was not sweet. It happened so fast. One second she was peeking over the opening, the next the horse had wheeled around, ears flat against its head, teeth bared, ready to take a chunk out of any part of her he could reach. It lunged for her and only Jace's quick action saved her from a vicious bite. A loud, angry scream from the horse followed the near miss.

For several moments, Kelly stood in Jace's arms, trying to slow her racing heart. She'd never had a close call with something that big and that vicious; she'd never been attacked by any animal. She turned her face into the soft, muscle-hugging T-shirt and deeply inhaled Jace's familiar scent as she fought to overcome the fright.

"Kelly, honey, are you all right?"

All she could do was nod. For a few minutes, Kelly stood in his embrace, feeling his strength and power, not wanting to step away.

"That was my fault." His chin rested on the top of her head while his large hand rubbed her back. "This is a stallion here for breeding. The crew is working on the stud barn, but it isn't ready yet. I should have warned you not to open this door. His...job...keeps him a little testy."

Kelly closed her eyes, letting the deep reverberation of Jace's voice calm her. Then, taking a deep breath, she stepped out of his arms and felt a chill that hadn't been there before.

"I should have realized it wasn't a filly by the sheer size of him." She looked at the gleaming black stallion, still aggressively pawing the ground, nostrils flaring, and couldn't help but shiver. That had been a close call. "He's beautiful, though."

She shifted her gaze to Jace's face. Hot fire blazed in his eyes. Despite knowing better, she wanted to walk into that flame until it singed every part of her. In that moment, she wanted Jace to put his arms back around her and hold her forever, consequences be damned.

His gaze held hers as his hands cupped her face. "Kelly," he whispered, his voice graveled and deep.

Every cell in her body screamed for his touch; her lips ached to say *yes*. But Kelly knew there was no future with Jace. He would go back to making his films. Back to the worldwide party scene that was his life. It was inevitable. The ranch was not his home. He'd even told her he'd bought it for some downtime. How could she walk into a situation knowing firsthand how it would end? She hadn't had that foresight before, but this time there was no excuse. And she was frightened. Of herself. Because she loved him. And her resolve to keep Jace at arm's length was weakening more every day.

She stepped back, out of his arms, and he let her go. She knew he could see the desire in her eyes, but she wouldn't say the words he wanted to hear. The words she longed to say.

One of the ranch hands came around the corner, his gaze taking in the two of them standing next to the stall. "Hey, Jace. Glad I caught you. Evening, ma'am."

Kelly gave a forced smile and nodded.

"Lee got the papers for that last colt you bought and said they didn't look right. He told me if I saw you to ask if you could stop by his place in the morning or give him a call."

While the two men talked, Kelly ambled on toward the back of the massive structure. Off to the right she heard something, a small sound coming out of one of the stalls. Curious, she walked in that direction, and the sound gradually got louder. It was a cat. Kelly opened the empty stall door and peeked inside. In the far corner, encased in shadows, a small gray-striped tabby lay on the straw.

"Hi, little one." It meowed in response and sat up. When it did, Kelly spotted more gray underneath where it had been lying. The cat was a female. And she had babies. Three tiny kittens, two gray, one gold, lay sleeping, cuddled together in the bed of straw. The mother showed no fear as she walked to Kelly and rubbed against her legs. Bending over, she ran her hand over the soft fur. Then felt the ribs. The cat was half starved.

Kelly lit out of the stall at a dead run, no second guessing, no consideration needed when an animal, especially a mother, needed help. She didn't slow when she passed Jace and the cowhand, still talking in the center of the isle.

"Kelly?"

"I'll be right back."

She ran out of the barn and down the path to the main house. Entering the kitchen, she grabbed milk from the fridge, and from the pantry, a tin of potted meat, a can of tuna and a breakfast bowl. Racing to the bathroom, she snatched two towels, deep pile and velvety soft. Dumping the food and bowl into one of the towels, she grabbed the carton of milk and ran back to the barn, again passing Jace and the cowboy. She couldn't help but notice a look of curiosity on their faces.

Kelly carefully lifted the kittens and placed them in the center of one of the towels. She folded the second one in half and spread it over the little indention in the hay before gently placing the babies back in the little nest. Mama cat was watching but voiced no concern, as if she understood the human was trying to help. Soon the little cat was enjoying her meat, milk and then some fresh water, eating as if she hadn't had food in a week. Which she probably hadn't.

Kelly felt exhilarated. To be able to help out such tiny, helpless little things in a place that, to them, must be so big and scary was a good feeling. It was with that glow of happiness she turned and saw Jace standing behind her.

He didn't speak for a long moment. "I take it we have guests?"

Kelly quickly shook her head. "Aren't they precious? The mother was so hungry, you can feel her ribs." The smile on her face wavered. "You don't mind, do you, Jace?"

He entered the stall and knelt down next to her, shaking his head. Reaching out, he stroked the cat's back, and then returned his gaze to Kelly. "So what's her name?"

Kelly was radiant. Her face glowed with the innocence of a child on Christmas morning. It was the first time since he'd been back he'd seen that smile and the sparkle in her eyes.

She chewed her bottom lip and damned if he didn't feel a surge of hot need in his groin.

"How about Jacemina? Or…"

"How about Cat?"

"No," she scolded in that you-should-be-ashamed mother's tone. "It has to be a real name. She deserves a real name."

"I had an aunt named Martha," Jace offered. Where that came from he would never know. "Mom's older sister."

"Martha." She said it out loud. He could see the name rolling around in her head. She looked up at him, grinning ear to ear. "It's perfect." And before he had time to let the idea soak in that he now had a cat named Martha who was, apparently, the proud mother of three, Kelly hurled herself toward him. His arms automatically went around her. "Thank you, Jace!"

Jace swallowed hard. Kelly was exactly where he wanted her to be. And she was happy and bubbling. Not because she was in his arms, but because she'd found a cat. His male pride took a hit, but hell, he'd take what he could get.

She finished her spontaneous hug and sat back on her heels. Her eyes moved over his face and a more intense look came into them.

"You're really a very sweet and kind person." She frowned, tilting her head. "I don't know if I ever realized that about you. It's not the same thing as being nice." Of her own volition, she leaned toward him. "Or sexy," she added, placing her lips against his.

His erection jumped to full attention. One arm pulled her closer while his other hand threaded through the silken strands of her long hair. He deepened the kiss, immediate need surging through his body.

"You taste so good," she murmured and he almost lost it. Right there in front of Martha Cat and her babies. Gently, Jace turned her into his arms, her head resting on his upper arm as he held her, his mouth never leaving hers. The moist heat of the kiss sent a shock wave rolling through him. His heart raced, showing no sign of slowing down anytime soon. Her hands cupped the sides of his face and for long moments he enjoyed the pure delight of her touch, the warmth of her body against his, every breath she took. Finally, reluctantly, he pulled back, knowing where they were headed and realizing it would embarrass her if one of the crew walked by.

As she lay in his arms, with her long hair falling over his sleeve and against his shirt, those blue-green eyes holding him spellbound, she reached up and played at his lower lip with her finger, exploring, bringing him to the edge of madness. With a slight movement, he took her finger inside his mouth, sucking, nipping lightly with his teeth. She was killing him. He wanted her beyond anything he'd ever wanted in his life.

"Who'd have thunk it?" She grinned, popped her finger out of his mouth and tapped him on the nose. "Tough guy Jace Compton is a mush melon inside. A sweet, kind man who rescues little kitties."

"Yeah," Jace muttered, reluctantly rising to his feet, pulling Kelly with him. "Who'd have thunk it?"

Ten

Together they headed back to the main house to get Henry. His mother did a double take when they walked into the den, laughing and clearly happy, Jace's arm around Kelly's shoulder. Henry was in the playpen next to where she sat on the sofa paging through fashion magazines.

"Has someone been playing in the hay?" Her smile of welcome turned into a grin of speculation. Her eyes twinkled.

Jace ran a hand through his hair, dislodging several twigs of straw. He then reached over and pulled some from Kelly's long strands.

"Sorry we're late," Kelly said as she walked over to give Mona a hug. "The horses are incredible. There's one that's the color of a copper penny. Mona, you must come out and see her. And the best part—we found *kittens*." She turned and looked at Jace, excitement lighting up her face. "Tell her, Jace."

"We found kittens."

"A mother and three tiny babies. She is almost starved. But I think she'll be okay. She is so sweet. I owe you and Jace for a can of tuna and milk."

"Not a problem, sweetheart. I love cats."

"So do I." Kelly reached for Henry. "Jace named her Martha."

"Did he?" There was a wicked light in her eyes. "Martha Compton. Who would have ever thought?"

"Aunt Martha hated my father," Jace dutifully explained,

seeing the confusion on Kelly's face. "The names Martha and Compton are not synonymous with any feelings remotely seen as warm and fuzzy. That should be a very strong cat." His mother chuckled and Jace leaned over and gave her a kiss on the cheek. "I'm going to walk Kelly back to the cabin."

"I won't wait up." She stood from the sofa. "You both have a good evening. Kelly, perhaps tomorrow you will take me to see the kittens?"

"Absolutely."

With Jace carrying Henry, they walked through the evening shadows to the small house in the trees. Jace followed her inside.

"Do you have time to hold him while I warm his bottle?"

"Sure." As Kelly headed to the kitchen, Jace wondered at the feel of his tiny son in his arms, the weight of his compact little body. It did strange things to Jace's heart. *His son.* He rubbed his face against the downy hair, loving the smell of baby powder, captivated by the little baby sounds. Henry's fist was again planted in his mouth, the sound of his lips smacking interspersed with words only Henry could understand. His head bobbled as he perched on his father's arm. Too soon he began to squirm and whimper.

"What's a matter, Henry?" No amount of coaxing would calm him down. "Kelly, is something wrong?" Jace asked in a concerned tone. "Is he sick?"

"Just hungry." Kelly came forward with the bottle. "Our little man has a very good appetite. Want to feed him?"

His eyes shot to her. It was an offer he hadn't expected. "Yeah. I'd like that."

"Find a seat."

Kelly found it hard to suppress a grin at Jace's intense expression. He sat down, still holding a fussing baby against his chest.

"You need to lay him back in your arms. Pretend he's a football," she suggested.

Nodding, Jace positioned Henry on his left arm, cuddled against his chest.

"Good." Kelly handed him the bottle.

Seeing Henry in his little blue rompers held so lovingly by his big tough dad caused her throat to constrict with emotion. She'd never let herself envision the picture in front of her. A small twinge of sadness touched her heart at the way fate had set their course adrift in different directions. Over the few weeks Jace had been back in her life and now seeing him like this, she knew he would be a great father. *If onlys* flooded her mind. But there was no going back. And there was no going forward. Not together. Destiny wasn't that kind.

Jace seemed to have fallen into a trance as he stared down at the baby in his arms. Henry took his bottle with gusto, his tiny hand gripping Jace's little finger.

"He's amazing," Jace murmured, and then gazed up at Kelly. "He looks just like you."

"No." She shook her head, quick to disagree. "He looks like *you*. Even has your dimples. I hope he doesn't become as bullheaded."

Jace made a huffing sound. She leaned against the wall, content to watch as Jace fed his son.

"I never intended to have kids," Jace said unexpectedly, his eyes glued on his son. "I never pictured a child in my life. Like you said, I'm gone more than I'm home. And even then, there's always something I have to do, something going on. It never stops. Meetings, overnight trips, PR campaigns… This is the longest I've ever managed to stay put."

She shrugged. He hadn't said anything she hadn't already suspected. "It's your job. It's what you do." *It's your choice.*

"Yeah." His tone was not happy. He glanced over at Kelly. "Do you think about his future? Who he will be? What he'll want to do with his life?"

"Every day."

Jace's gaze returned to the baby in his arms. The look on

Jace's face was intense. It was as though his mind had taken him to another place. And not necessarily a good place.

"He's so amazing. From his fingers to his toes…he's perfect. And so innocent." He watched Henry slurp on his evening feeding. After a few long moments, Jace's gaze returned to Kelly. "I don't understand people who would ever hurt a child," he blurted out.

Kelly's eyes widened in surprise. Where did that come from? Had Jace witnessed abuse at some point in his past? Might that be a reason Jace didn't want a family?

"There are all kinds of people, Jace," she said gently, wanting to take away the misery in his expression. "You above all know that, with the oddball fans you have to deal with. You just have to make sure to keep your child safe and well away from any potential harm. That's just part of the job of being a father."

She saw his jaw muscles clench. He nodded and swallowed hard.

"Yeah." Then he seemed to realize the path his mind was on and changed the subject. "When did your grandfather pass away?"

"Um…about a week after you left."

"Was he sick very long?"

"No. Some developers were after his farm and I think he was really stressed over that. They claimed his title was invalid. I came home from school the week after New Year's and found him. He'd had a massive stroke. By the time the paramedics got there it was too late. A letter of eviction was on the floor next to him."

She couldn't stop the sudden rush of moisture that burned her eyes. She lowered her head, hoping Jace wouldn't notice.

"What happened to your parents, if you don't mind my asking?"

It was Kelly's turn to take a few minutes to formulate her answer. She hadn't expected the question, didn't quite know what to say and wasn't at all sure she wanted to go there. It had been a really great evening, and talking about her parents was jumping off a very high cliff with no possibility of a good outcome at the bottom. Finally, she decided to leave off the sugarcoating and tell him the truth. Let him read into it what he would.

"My father, apparently, wasn't happy at home. Like you, he traveled a lot. But even when he was home, there were other women. Lots of other women. A couple of them were the mothers of my classmates. *That* was fun."

Jace frowned. "How do you mean?"

"My classmates blamed me for breaking up their homes..." It wasn't something she wanted to remember. "Gossip was rampant. The stories grew bigger and bigger. It...it was a tough time for us." Her dad was the playboy of the year if the rumor mill was to be believed. But Kelly didn't say it out loud. What good could come of it? "Mom refused to leave him. She just numbed her pain with liquor and pills. She finally got the right combination when I was sixteen." Tears sprang to Kelly's eyes. She put her hand over her mouth, taking a few seconds to get her emotions under control. She rubbed the tears away and blinked hard. "Sorry. Anyway, Dad came to the funeral, but we never saw him again after that."

"*Damn.* I'm sorry, Kelly."

She shrugged. "He didn't care. He wasn't meant to be married. All he wanted was a good time. Gramps was a kind man and we loved him. I hate to think what might have happened had he not stepped forward and taken us in. I finished high school, got a student loan, started at the university and for a while, life went on. Until he died. Then it was Matt and me against the world." She had to smile. "I think we did pretty good. You couldn't ask for a better brother, but don't you dare tell Matt I said that." *Keep it light. Grit your teeth and get through this.*

She'd lost her parents because her father was a two-faced cheating bastard who was too spineless to end the mar-

riage. Her mother had been too weak to leave him. She'd
lost Gramps after a wealthy man and his high-priced attorneys found or fabricated a loophole in the deed and took
his farm. And here she sat, smack in the middle of a lion's
den, Jace being both a philanderer and as wealthy as they
come. She'd given birth to his baby and already experienced the temptation to return to his bed. She was as big a
fool as her mother.

The silence that filled the room was deafening. Gone
was the lighthearted camaraderie from earlier. It would be
so easy to let the rest of the tears fall. But she refused. The
very last thing she wanted was Jace's pity. She had to wonder if he saw the similarities between him and her father. At
least Jace hadn't gotten married before he'd begun *chasing
the skirts*, as Gramps used to call it. He'd never had anything good to say about Kelly's father. She couldn't help
but speculate what her grandpa would have thought of Jace.

The loud sound of Henry sucking on an empty bottle
suddenly filled the room.

"I think he's finished." She stepped forward and took
the bottle, glad for the interruption.

"What's next?"

Kelly placed a cloth over Jace's shoulder. "Hold him up-
right next to your chest. Be careful to support his head. Put
one hand under his butt and gently pat his back with the
other. Just pretend your favorite starlet needs consoling."

Jace shot her a warning glance, and then wrestled Henry
around until he was against his shoulder. It was a sight to
behold. Jace's hand was as big as Henry's entire back. But
his touch was gentle, as though Henry were so fragile he
might break. In fact, Jace was only patting the folds of
Henry's shirt.

"You're gonna need to pat him a little harder if you want
to get that bubble out." The look Jace gave her was something close to panic. Some tabloid would pay big bucks for
a picture of this. "It's okay, Jace. He won't break."

Jace nodded and tried again. After considerable time had passed, Henry turned his head toward his father and appeared to nuzzle his neck. Seconds later, Kelly heard the burp. It was followed by a small stream of milk. Completely missing the cloth, it trickled down Jace's thick neck and into his shirt.

He looked up at Kelly, and the expression on his face was priceless. She hurried to take the baby.

"He's been a little fussy today. Teething. Sorry about that."

Jace cleared his throat and stood up. "No problem."

"He's ready for his bath and then bed."

"I think I know the feeling." He stood and reached for his shirt, pulling the wet material away from his neck.

Kelly bit her lip to keep from laughing. "Bath time can be fun."

"I couldn't agree more with you there," he said, his eyes glinting wickedly. "Baths and showers can be an amazingly good time."

Heat rushed up her neck. He was not talking about bathing a baby. She knew only too well what Jace could do with a bar of soap and a little warm water.

"But this time I think I'll pass." Jace stopped before he stepped outside, still holding his collar away from his skin. "Thanks for...this, Kelly."

"Sure." She covered her mouth with her hand in an effort to hold back a giggle. From smiles to tears and back to laughter. Such was a day spent in the presence of Jace Compton.

Jace followed the path back to the main house, his mind spinning, his gut churning. He and Kelly had been together only weeks before her grandfather died. At a time when she needed him the most, he was twelve hundred miles away listening to Bret tell him lies about her, insisting Jace not call her as he'd promised. By the day of the funeral, he'd been on his way to South America for a film shoot.

He rubbed the back of his neck, a sinking feeling in his gut. A man couldn't get a whole lot lower. He hadn't known her circumstances, but he should have called her before he ever boarded that plane. It explained so much: why she'd left school, why she worked two jobs, why she had to support Matt and her baby. Why, when he'd come to his senses and tried to call, the phone had been disconnected. No wonder she resented him. Hell. She had every right. It was a miracle she didn't hate him.

Did she think he was just like her father?

The thought sent a sickening surge through his body. His actions toward her so far, combined with the bullshit facade he had to perpetuate for the public... Yeah. He could see how she would. And there was not one damn thing he could do to change it.

He respected Kelly for her strength and tenacity. But he knew firsthand how fast that strength could fly out the window when facing down a cruel, vicious adversary twice your size: an intoxicated man determined to hurt you and your child. That his mother had survived and managed to hide them and keep them safe when his father got out of prison was nothing short of a miracle.

Not for the first time, Jace cursed his fate. Having Kelly and Henry here, seeing them, interacting with them, was everything he'd ever longed for. A perfect family. One he could never have. He'd been serious the day he'd told Kelly if she was concerned about public speculation to marry him. But she'd been right when she called him on it. A marriage between them could never last. But not for the reasons she thought. It had nothing to do with Henry. It was because there was a monster inside him, a monster that could hurt Kelly and the baby. Marriage would work fine on paper. Put the gossips to rest. But a real marriage and family, for him, could never happen.

Kelly was a temptation to which he'd become addicted.

He wanted her until it hurt; it was almost unbearable torment every time she came near.

He had to get a handle on it.

Kelly deserved a man who could give her forever. A guy who would pamper her and protect her, not turn on her someday. Not only had his old man convinced Jace he was worthless and then died before Jace could prove him wrong, he'd ensured, even after he was dead and buried, that his son's life was on a direct downhill course to hell.

Eleven

"I'll be damned," Jace muttered under his breath as he leaned out over the railing. They were grilling something. One of the cowboys had rolled in an outdoor grill from God knows where and they were actually grilling food—maybe hot dogs?—just outside of Kelly's cabin. Jace squinted to get a better look. There were binoculars in the study downstairs, but he refused to stoop to that level. Yet.

From the balcony outside his bedroom, he had a fairly clear view of the front of her little house. He'd first noticed the Friday night gathering three weeks ago. He'd heard laughter coming from that direction and stepped outside, wondering who it was and what could be so damned funny.

At first he'd seen old Sam, the ranch foreman, Decker and another trainer sitting out on the tiny porch with Kelly. The next weekend, he'd given into curiosity and looked again. This time they'd been joined by at least a half dozen cowboys, sitting on crates, laughing the night away. Even Matt later joined the party. The little group had grown until now almost every unmarried hand working on the ranch sat circled around that porch. And in the middle of all those lonesome, lusting, hungry men sat the princess bee herself. Kelly drew them like a budding flower, and every drone in the county wanted to get close in spite of the fact that some nights she bounced the baby on her lap. *His* baby. She'd invited him to stop by but he had no wish to join the crowd while they sat and ogled Kelly. It was none of his concern, but at the same time he fought the overwhelming urge to go down there and beat the living crap out of any one of the bastards who tried to put the moves on her.

Adding to his frustration was the knowledge that he'd been the one who had convinced her to move to the little house. He'd wanted her to be close. He'd never considered he wouldn't be the only one she would be close to.

And now they were cooking for her. *Dammit to hell.*

"Jace?" his mother called from inside his room. He turned and headed in that direction. If she caught a glimpse of the goings-on at the little cottage and him leaning over the balcony railing, she might get the wrong idea.

"What are you doing?"

Why did he suddenly feel like a ten-year-old who'd gotten caught with his hand in the cookie jar? He stepped inside and closed the door behind him. "Just getting some fresh air. What's up? Are you okay?"

"Oh, I'm fine. I was just curious if you'd gone to the party."

He couldn't miss the mischievous light dancing in her eyes. "Party?"

"The one at Kelly's cabin."

Damn. "I didn't know about any party."

"Uh-huh. Well, I'm sure you'd be welcome. Why don't you go down and join them?"

The last thing he wanted to do was be yet another bee blazing a trail to Kelly's sweet nectar. "I'm really kinda busy. Need to read the new script. I don't have time to go to a party."

"Right." Turning, she walked toward the door. "Whatever you say. Just wanted to let you know I'm going out this evening."

"Out? Where? With who?"

"Thomas—Dr. Sullivan—invited me to have dinner. He should be here anytime."

"Oh." Jace felt a twinge of uneasiness mixed with surprise. Granted, Sullivan was the town doctor who commanded a certain amount of respect, but what did they really know about him? Jace couldn't prevent visions of his father's fist slamming into her delicate jaw time after time from flashing through his mind. His instinct to protect her was strong. He supposed he should try to remember his mother was, after all, an adult. And the doctor wasn't his father. Still, Jace gritted his teeth. "I don't suppose you'd consider letting one of the security team——"

"Absolutely not."

He nodded. "Well, then have a good time."

"I intend to." She winked and turned toward the door to his suite. "Oh," she said over her shoulder, "the binoculars are in the desk in your office downstairs if they would help with your...work. Bye-bye."

Jace pulled both hands through his hair. Dammit to hell. He had to get a grip on this Kelly thing. He'd become like a daytime barn owl, practically living in the office in the main stable in an attempt to stay away from the house as much as possible. When he did give it up and return to the house, it was straight to the gym or his office to check emails. The new script had arrived, but it sat unread on his desk; Jace had found neither the concentration nor the motivation to even open the mailing envelope. Something had to change or he could plan on spending the rest of his nights pacing the balcony like some seriously messed-up loser.

It was impossible to treat Kelly as just a friend. He refused to be just another of the drooling, lusting men clustering around her. His body knew she was his and responded accordingly regardless of the time and place.

Kelly was the only one who ever came close to being *the* woman in his life. He'd been with beautiful women. He'd known women with kindness in their hearts. But Kelly had that unique something, that special quality that brought it all together. She was in a league of her own. A treasure that remained out of reach.

Jace suspected part of what had kept him from coming

back sooner was a deep-seated fear he was getting too in-volved with her. He'd begun picturing them together. For-ever. He hadn't been prepared for that. And in light of the monster he might someday become, it had frightened him.

But now, over a year later, things had changed. He had a son. And he was still as infatuated with Kelly as he'd ever been. What would happen if he risked it? Kept her in his life? The idea was making him crazy.

Sleeping with another woman was not appealing. But if he persisted and seduced Kelly, he might hurt her someday. It was a hell of a dilemma.

A wave of laughter from outside drifted into the room. *Dammit to hell.*

"C Bar Ranch," Kelly said into the phone.

On Monday Jace asked her to take on the additional duty of answering his private line. Lee arrived with new horses and everyone was running in high gear. At least that was the excuse. Whether Kelly believed it was still open to speculation. Initially the calls went to his voice mail, but by Monday afternoon, that was full. Now, three days later, the calls were coming in fast and furious and Jace had yet to clear them from his phone. No surprise there.

"Just see if you can help them," he'd instructed. "Take their names and numbers. I'll call them back later. If it sounds urgent, try to page me."

They all sounded urgent. Kelly didn't like it. She didn't want to know who called him, hated talking to the smug-sounding women, but she hadn't come up with an accept-able reason to refuse. Yet.

"I have Joanna Reed calling for Jace Compton." The woman's voice was pleasant and professional. A nice change from most of the other callers.

"I'm sorry. Mr. Compton is not currently available. Per-haps I can help you?"

"No. Thank you. Miss Reed must speak directly with Mr. Compton. It's urgent she reach him as soon as possible."

Of course it was. "One moment, please. I'll try and page him." *Urgent* was the magic word. Kelly placed the call on hold and punched the intercom for the barn office. "Jace, you have a call on line one," she said, using their code for his private phone.

There was no answer. *Surprise. Surprise.*

"Jace, if you're there, please pick up."

"Kelly, this is Lee. Jace headed back to the house an hour ago. Don't know what to tell you past that."

"Okay. Thanks."

She punched the button for the house intercom. "Jace, a Miss Joanna Reed is holding on your private line." After waiting several seconds, Kelly returned to the caller. "I'm sorry. Mr. Compton isn't answering the page. Would you care to leave a message?"

She heard voices in the background, and then another voice came on the line.

"This is Joanna Reed. What is the problem?"

"As I've explained to your secretary, Mr. Compton is not near a phone. I'll be happy to take a—"

Her end of the conversation had caught Mona's attention. The older woman stood and walked toward Kelly's desk. Kelly put the call on speaker. Might as well share the wealth.

"Then find him. This is outrageous."

"I'm sorry, Ms. Reed. I seem to have lost the ability to make someone appear by snapping my fingers or twitching my nose. I'll be sure to get that checked. Again, I'll be glad to take your number."

"Do you honestly think he doesn't have it?"

"I really wouldn't know."

Kelly looked at Mona. This was ridiculous. Mona put her slender hand over her mouth to stifle a laugh as her shoulders began to shake.

"Will there be anything else?"

"Just one thing. I will reach Jace eventually and you might as well start packing up your things. You are gone."

"I appreciate the early notification."

"You can also tell Jace the next time he…needs me… I'll be busy. And the fault will be yours."

"Have a nice day."

Kelly terminated the call. Mona and Jace paid her well, but not nearly enough to take that crap.

"I'm not doing this," she said to Mona with as much calm as she could muster. It was the hundredth such call in the past three days, each one progressively worse than the last. Crazy women. Acting as if they owned Jace Compton.

"You might try the gym," Mona said, an impish twinkle in her eyes.

"Thanks." Kelly stomped out of the room and headed for the first-floor gym.

When she rounded the corner, sure enough, Jace was lying on a bench, his hands gripping a barbell with several weights on either end, straining to push it up and down. Beads of sweat ran down his face and neck, his biceps ballooning to an enormous size. She didn't want to startle him and cause an accident, so she stood next to the wall and waited. The man who usually flew in and trained with him every few days was not here. Should Jace be doing this alone?

Finally, he set the heavy bar on the rack and sat up. Grabbing a towel hanging nearby, he wiped his face and neck.

She cleared her throat. Jace saw her for the first time and tilted his head with a surprised look.

"Kelly?"

"I refuse to answer your phone. I *refuse*," she repeated, leaning forward, her hands perched at her waist.

His eyebrows rose. "Okay. Mind telling me why?"

"Like you don't know." She couldn't hold back a sarcastic laugh. "Do you have any idea how many lunatics call you in a day? Never mind. Of course you do. That's why you stuck me with the job. Then you refuse to answer my page and I'm the one who gets attacked."

"Attacked?" He stood up from the bench. His ragged cutoffs rode low on his waist and molded to the muscular hips and thighs. That's all he was wearing. The tanned flesh of his muscled chest and flat stomach glistened with perspiration.

Good Lord. Couldn't the man put on some clothes?

"They think I'm lying to them. Cherry Newton has called four times. Today. Do people make up these names? That sounds like a sandwich cookie you'd pull off a tree. She's threatening to have me arrested, insinuating I must have done something to you to keep you from talking to her. Cora Spager—Stagler —has called ten times. *Ten.* The last call, I had to sit and listen to her alternately rage and cry for almost an hour. I just got off the phone with the Wicked Witch of the West, who said I should tell you the next time you *needed* her—" Kelly made a snorting sound "—she wouldn't be available and it was entirely my fault. How exactly is it *my* fault? Oh, she also said that I should be forewarned—this is my last day of employment. Finally, some good news."

Kelly noted the grin he was trying to hide, and her irritation doubled. "This is not funny, Jace. Your idiotic calls are taking my time away from Mona and making me crazy."

"I'm sorry." The wicked glitter in his eyes told her he was not sorry at all. His spicy male scent was strong from his workout, and her body responded to the sight of his sculpted chest, sweaty and gleaming. She tried to swallow but her mouth had gone dry.

"Then hire an agency. Use a call center," she said in a ragged voice, then tried to clear her throat, fighting the response of her traitorous body. "But don't expect me to bite my lip while those ladies, and I use the term loosely, call me every name in the book."

As soon as she said the word *lip*, his eyes focused on that part of her face.

"Say no more." He moved closer. "Because no one is going to bite those lips but me."

"Jace." She began to back out of the room, shaking her head. "I'm serious."

"So am I."

"Don't do this."

"You feel it, too."

The husky timbre of his voice told her he sensed the change in her. She'd made a huge mistake coming to the gym. She fought to maintain her poise, taking calm, steady breaths. *Just get out of here.*

A smile played at the corners of his full lips. "I think you want me...to kiss you again."

Yes. "No." She again cleared her throat. "No, I don't." It was almost a whisper. Another step away from him and she felt the wall against her back. A heady sexual tension mixed with a touch of panic enveloped her.

"I damn sure want to kiss you. Hell, I want to do a lot more than that."

"Jace..."

He looped the small towel around his neck and placed his hands against the wall on either side of her head, his huge biceps bulging. She felt the coolness against her back, a vivid contrast to the smoldering heat radiating from him.

"It's making me crazy having you here, seeing you every day and never touching you."

Bending down, he placed his warm mouth against the very place under her ear he knew caused sweet shivers to run through her. She couldn't repress a little cry as her eyes closed and her skin sizzled. Her hands came up against his granite chest and she felt the strong steady beat of his heart.

"Kelly." His intonation was so deep, so mesmerizing, he held her captive using nothing more than his voice.

"You don't play fair," she murmured against his lips,

which were so tantalizingly close. She sounded breathy to her own ears. "We shouldn't do this."

"Who are you trying to convince? Me or yourself? Admit it, Kelly. Say you want me and let's stop this damned cat-and-mouse game."

"I don't think—"

"Good. I don't want you to think. Just go with your feelings."

With a small whimper, Kelly leaned forward, moving her lips even closer to his, seeking the pleasure she knew was there. Jace didn't wait a full heartbeat before his mouth took hers, fiercely, deeply, his tongue filling every crevice. "Say it, Kelly," he groaned, before kissing her again, intensely, with such passion she couldn't have spoken had she wanted to. She heard him growl, and his mouth opened wider, hungrily, as though he couldn't get enough.

Kelly was lost. She couldn't fight this. No one could. It was as though the power of the mythical god Zeus surged through him, proving that all the stories of his erotic escapades were true. Mere mortal women didn't stand a chance. Jace's arms came around her, pulling her closer to his hard frame. His arousal pressed against her belly, and like a branding iron, it singed her skin through her clothes, making sure she knew she was his. She couldn't stop the small moan forming deep in her throat, but it was swallowed by his hungry mouth.

His big hands slid under her hips, lifting her, pulling her tightly against him, making her feel his body's reaction to her, his heavy thickness leaving no doubt what he wanted. She wanted the same. She needed to feel him against her core with shameless intensity.

"Jace?"

A distant voice broke into the moment.

"Hey man, you in the gym?" The head trainer called out from the den, no doubt heading in their direction.

Jace lifted his head and stared into her eyes. "Someday

very soon, your luck is going to run out." He stepped back and dropped his arms. "Yeah," he called out to Lee, still holding her with his gaze.

"I'll make a deal with you, Kelly. Stop the damn Friday night smorgasbord and I'll take care of the phone calls."

Her mouth dropped open. "*That's* what answering your phone is about?" Jace saw her visiting with some of the ranch hands…and he was *jealous*? Jace Compton? The man wasn't jealous of anyone or anything on the planet. He could have any woman he wanted. But the aroused hunk standing two feet in front of her appeared deadly serious. "They are just a few nice cowboys who—"

"Who would take you to their bed in a heartbeat. You're the mother of *my* child," he snarled as if she didn't know that.

"And your point is?"

Jace's eyes narrowed, his nostrils flaring with emotion. "If you need sex, you come to me."

He did not just say that. "I'll tell you what, Compton. You hold your breath until that happens. See how that works for you."

With a last glare, Kelly turned and stomped to the door, colliding smack into the trainer as she rounded the corner. Only Lee's quick reflexes kept her from falling on her butt.

Her mind was blown. The very idea that Jace could ever be envious of the men on the ranch was just not believable. She was an employee in his house, which made her a convenience. That's all it was. He needed to get out of the house for a few days. He needed to be reminded there was an entire world waiting for him outside the boundaries of this ranch and that world was filled with beautiful, desirable women who would do anything to be with him. To say he was a very potent package was an understatement. And the idea that he could be in any way jealous… It was too much to take in.

It took a good part of the afternoon to push Jace's antics

in the gym out of her mind. With Henry napping and Mona there to watch him, Kelly finally went downstairs, gathered a can of cat food and a couple of apples, and headed for the barn. The need to make love with Jace again, to feel his hands and body work their magic, was eating her up inside. She might as well admit defeat. It didn't matter what she felt for him, be it mere physical attraction or something more: he was dangerous. In every single way that mattered. And that enticing element, in itself, would be her undoing.

Wednesday evening Kelly had just settled Henry for the night when there was a knock on the door. One of the ranch hands stood on the porch, his hat in his hands. Kelly remembered meeting him the day she'd moved in.

"Decker?"

"Evening, Kelly. Are you busy?"

"No." She shook her head. "I just put the baby to bed."

"They're having a barn dance at the Bar H spread to celebrate the birth of their daughter. I was curious if you were going and if you might need a ride."

"No, I mean, I didn't know anything about it. Shea and I haven't talked in months."

"Well, I realize it's late notice. I just found out about it myself. It's only intended for the employees and family, but I remember you saying you and Shea were close. I doubt they will mind if you crash the party."

"Oh, I'd love to go," she said, the idea of seeing her friend again immediately taking root. "But I don't have anyone to keep my son. Unless…" *Would Mona watch him for a couple of hours?* "I can ask Mona if she'll sit with the baby. How long did you plan to stay?"

"That's entirely up to you."

Stepping inside, she grabbed the cell off the kitchen counter and dialed Mona's private line. She answered in two rings. After Kelly explained what she needed, Mona enthusiastically agreed.

"I'll bring Henry to the house in just a few minutes. Thank you, Mona."

Decker grinned when she told him she had a babysitter.

"How about if I pick you up in front of the main house in about ten minutes?"

"Perfect."

It would be so great to see Shea again. They hadn't had a chance to visit in far too long. Between Kelly working two jobs and having a new baby to care for and Shea and Alec spending the summer in Europe, the opportunity just hadn't been there. She grabbed the baby bag, gathered a sleeping Henry in her arms and hurried to the main house, excitement at seeing her old friend quickening her steps.

She didn't see Jace as she climbed the stairs to Mona's suite. In fact, she hadn't seen him that day at all. She didn't know if he had as yet met Shea and her husband but maybe he would like to go. Mona was waiting at the top of the stairs, her arms reaching out to take the baby into her arms.

"Do you know where Jace is?"

"He's in Dallas talking with some people about a new film."

"Oh." So much for that idea. "Okay then. I'll see you later. Thanks so much for doing this, Mona."

Decker was waiting when she came back downstairs and they were on their way to the Bar H.

"Wow," Decker said as he turned his truck into the long, rambling driveway of Shea's ranch. "That's some house."

"Shea's husband, Alec, is an architect and builder. Shea was devastated when her old ranch house burned down. Alec went over and above when he built their new home." The sprawling three-story Victorian-style house with its turret towers and four chimneys peeking over the high roof was the talk of three counties.

"I guess. Man."

They pulled into the designated parking area. Kelly heard the music and laughter as soon as she opened her door. The aroma of mesquite logs burning in the large grill tempted all to come and bring their plate.

"I think I see Shea over there." Decker pointed to a huge oak tree. "Go ahead and say hello and I'll catch up with you later."

"Thanks, Decker." Kelly raced to where Shea sat in a lawn chair.

"Shea?"

"Oh my gosh. Kelly!" Shea rose to her feet and the two friends embraced. "It's so great to see you."

"Same here. You look so good."

"Let's get you a chair. I want to know everything that's been happening. How are Matt and Henry?"

"They're good." Kelly grinned as she pulled a vacant chair next to Shea's. "I'm so happy for you. Congratulations on your new baby."

"Thanks. I want you to see her before you leave."

"I would love to. How is Alec handling being the dad to a little girl?"

Shea rolled her eyes. "She has him rolled around her little finger. You'd think she was the only baby girl ever born." It was wonderful talking with Shea and the time passed much too quickly. Too soon it was time to go. But Shea wouldn't let her leave without seeing her new baby.

"Come meet Alexandra Christine." Shea led the way across the yard and into the house. After a short tour of the magnificent home, they went up the staircase to the nursery where a sitter sat reading. Shea lifted the infant from the crib.

"Oh, Shea. She's beautiful. She looks just like you!"

"That's what Alec says. I've never seen a man go totally off the deep end over a baby. He hired a nurse for the first six weeks, then questioned everything she said or did. After a few days he decided he knew what his daughter needed better than she did. I think her leaving was by mutual agreement."

Kelly smiled but was suddenly struck with the hopelessness of her own situation. To have Jace always around every day to watch his son grow and develop into a fine man was a dream Kelly kept locked away deep inside. She'd long ago accepted it would never happen. But in moments like this, she couldn't stop the hope from breaking free, only to have it wither and die in the chill of reality.

"It's so great we're neighbors now," Shea was saying. "You've gotta come over when you have time. Bring Henry."

Kelly nodded, not trusting her voice. If Shea noticed that she'd suddenly became quiet she said nothing. She just leaned over and gave Kelly a hug.

Outside, Kelly easily spotted Decker. When she approached him, his grin faded and he frowned in concern. She tried to smile but Decker apparently sensed something was wrong and asked if she was ready to leave. Was she that transparent? Not good.

"Thank you so much, Decker," she said as they made their back to his truck.

"No problem. I'm glad you got to see your friend." Decker was a nice guy, and with his blond hair and good looks, he certainly wasn't hard on the eyes. But he wasn't Jace.

She slipped from his truck and entered the house. Walking through the kitchen, she headed for the stairs, not bothering to turn on any lights. There was enough radiant light spilling into the house for her to see where she was going.

Before she reached the room Mona had deemed as a temporary nursery, a dark shadow on the left moved toward her. Kelly barely held in a shriek.

"Did you have a good night?"

"Jace. You scared me." What was he doing standing in a darkened hallway? "Yes. I did, thank you."

She moved forward but Jace stepped in front of her, blocking her way. Through the dim glow of the night-light Mona insisted on having at the top of the stairs, she could see he was dressed in only a pair of old jeans. And he wasn't smiling.

"I wasn't aware you were dating anyone."

Did he really have any right to know if she was or wasn't? How rude would it be to just keep walking?

She shrugged. "I'm not." She gave him that much and tried to step around him, wanting to get Henry and go to her cabin. Jace again blocked her way.

"That's not what it looked like to me."

Oh, here we go. Mr. Macho was back.

"You don't consider going out with Decker a date?" Jace continued.

"He gave me a ride to the Bar H," she explained, forcing her voice to remain calm. "Shea just had her baby a couple of weeks ago. Their ranch crew honored her and her husband with a party. They had a barbecue. It wasn't a date. And you weren't here. I asked Mona, thinking you might like to go. Do you know Shea and her husband, Alec?" No answer. "Do you know their ranch hands?" No answer. She'd take bets he was clenching his teeth.

Again she attempted to step to the side and continue on her way. And again, Jace blocked her path.

"Decker has a reputation, Kelly."

"So do you." She was starting to get angry.

"Did he kiss you?"

She glared at him, refusing to answer.

He rubbed the back of his neck, before meeting her gaze across the short space that separated them. "Do you think about us, Kelly? About those three weeks when we first met?" he asked in a low, husky tone.

Her heart increased in tempo. If only he knew.

Twelve

"Do you ever think about the time we spent together?"

"I... Jace, don't do this." She shook her head. Her emotions were already raw, splintered. After seeing Shea's baby and again facing the reality of her own situation, she felt as if she'd been pulled inside out, every nerve in her body scraped raw. Before her stood the man who had given her the world. Then taken it away.

"I think about it," he said as though needing her to know.

Something inside her snapped. "Then why didn't you call?" The unfairness suddenly overwhelmed her and she almost screamed the words as she blinked back angry tears. "Why didn't you come back? I will not be a convenience, Jace. I'll never again be simply a diversion to relieve some rich man's boredom. Now please let me by."

"You were never just a diversion. Dammit, Kelly."

He pulled her hard against him, his hot mouth coming down over hers. For a few seconds, she fought to be free of his arms, pushing against his wide shoulders, crying on the inside as she fought the overwhelming need to embrace him.

This was Jace. This was the man she loved. His lips, his scent, his voice, the feel of his powerful arms holding her firmly but gently, was what she'd longed for all those many months. This was the never-ending dream that came to her on those nights when she was too weak to push it away.

With a small desperate whimper of defeat, she gave in to her weakness, clutched the front of his shirt and opened her lips, letting him in. She kissed him back with an urgency propelled by the torturous need that had ripped at her soul for so many months. No longer held in check, the bittersweet memories pummeled the last remaining bits of her resolve. She gloried in his kiss once again, warmed by the heat of his body, his hard erection pressing against her stomach. His hungry mouth devoured hers as he pulled her closer. She felt his heart beating as fast as her own as his tongue explored the recesses of her mouth, enticing hers to do the same. His hands moved to cup her face, holding her to his, and she heard him moan.

He swept her into his arms and carried her into his bedroom and kicked the door closed behind them. Not breaking the kiss, Jace set her down next to the bed and made quick work removing her blouse. She absently felt him remove her bra, felt the cool air on her skin as his hands cupped her, squeezing gently, his thumbs playing across the sensitive nubs, making them harden under his touch. Bending down, he took one firm nipple into his mouth, sucking gently. Kelly moaned at the exquisite pleasure. Her back arched, her breasts swelled under his touch. He moved to the other breast, giving it the same attention. She heard the faint sound of a zipper being opened and her jeans were pushed down and over her hips. Then his mouth returned to hers and Kelly became lost in the sensation, in the gut-wrenching need overtaking her. Fisting her hands in his hair, she held on as the room began to spin. She felt a floating sensation, and then absently realized she was in his bed, covers thrown back, her jeans tugged from her legs.

He used his knee to ease her legs apart, and then settled on top of her. His hard erection pushed almost painfully, urgently against her core. His breath was hot against her skin as he kissed her neck, slowly moving to her ear, nipping and kissing her jaw before returning to her mouth.

A white-hot flow of heat coursed through her body, building into an unrelenting fire at the apex of her thighs. Her need reached a frantic level as she twisted, trying to adjust her position and take him inside. He was breathing hard as his lips and tongue continued to feed, the sheer heat of his mouth making her want to embrace him, to give in to what they both wanted.

Kelly was out of her mind. Her hips arched against him, conveying her need. She wanted to feel more of Jace. Inside her. Filling her.

Jace unzipped his jeans and let them fall. He felt a long-forgotten tingle at the base of his spine and knew he had to get inside her, fast. She was so damned hot he was going to lose it. Grabbing some protection from the drawer in his nightstand, he quickly put it in place. With Kelly, it had always been like this: a raw, gripping, almost unquenchable need that made them frantic in their actions to unite as one. With one hand, he tested her, two fingers pressed inside, eliciting a soft moan.

"Are you ready for me, Kelly?" he murmured against her ear.

Her body arched against his hand, silently conveying her need. With the pulse hammering in his veins he covered her, positioned his shaft at her core and experienced that tingle again, this time radiating up his spine, splintering his mind. Any illusions that he could take it slow went up in flames as he pushed his heavy length inside, filling her…

Sweat broke out on Jace's forehead and he knew taking this easy was not going to happen. With a rough growl, he pushed still deeper, unable to completely absorb the almost painful pleasure of the throbbing heat that encased him.

"Are you okay?"

She gave a partial nod and pulled his mouth back to hers.

As he began to move, she moaned, biting his lower lip, her hands gripping his back, attempting to hold him to her, expressing the same intense need that ran through him. His lips covered hers, his tongue filling her, simulating what was happening below.

Faster. Deeper. More intense. Until Jace lost hold on reality. He gripped her hips, raising her to him, and pushed even deeper. He rolled his hips and her head fell back against the pillow, her open mouth sending a clear message needing no words. As he took them to the next plane, he returned to the temptations of her lips and she drew his tongue inside, sucking hard. Jace's control snapped. He began to pummel against her, thrusting deeper and deeper with every stroke. He was going to lose it. Suddenly, Kelly stilled and cried out, all the air leaving her body as she arched up against him, shattering in raw pleasure. Her body clenching around him pushed Jace over the top. He couldn't hold back his own ragged moan as the intensity of his release overtook him, pulsating deep within her, spasm after spasm as if there were no end.

It seemed to take a millennium before the stars began to drift back down and settle in his totally shattered brain. His body lost its grip on whatever strength remained. Overwhelmed with heady weakness, he dropped to his side.

His hands found her face and he kissed her softly, loving the scent, the taste that was only Kelly. He felt her tremble as she kissed him back.

She was his.

"Did I hurt you?" he asked against her lips.

Her answer was a smile against his lips and a soft moan in the key of *no*.

The next morning, Kelly worked on the correspondence, logging the RSVPs for the charity gala and responding to both those who would be coming and, as a courtesy, those who would not.

She felt as though Mona could somehow tell what had happened between her son and Kelly just by looking at her face. Therefore, Kelly made every attempt not to look at Mona, turning a different direction if the older woman came into the doorway of her small office. If Mona noticed anything amiss, she chose to say nothing. But it wasn't Kelly's imagination that Jace's mom was smiling more than normal. But Kelly was, too; hopefully Mona didn't catch on.

The work was steady throughout the day. The detailed to-do list for the charity ball required Kelly's concentration, which kept her from reexperiencing the sensations brought by Jace's hands the night before. At least a little.

"Penny for your thoughts..." said a deep voice in her ear.

Kelly jumped and looked up to find the very subject of her thoughts directly in front of her. Bracing his hands on the edge of the small desk, Jace leaned toward her and raised his eyebrows, a small sexy smile on his full lips. She could feel the blush spread over her face.

Before she could respond, she heard Matt's voice call out, followed by footsteps running up the stairs. He entered the room in a full run.

"Kelly. Oh. Hi, Jace. Mrs. Compton." He was grinning from ear to ear. "Guess what happened today? You're never gonna believe it!" He was barely able to contain his enthusiasm. "Frank Gentry broke his leg during football practice!"

Kelly stared at him as though he'd lost his mind. She glanced at Mona, who had a curious look on her face. Jace straightened and placed his hands on his hips, as if waiting for more.

"This is *not* good news, Matt."

"Wait—his dad told Coach Hager he'll probably be out for the rest of the season. The coach talked to me privately and asked me to take his place. Oh, man. It's the *varsity* team, Kelly. I'll be the only sophomore on it."

"Oh my gosh. That's great, Matt." She jumped up from her chair and gave her brother a hug.

"Absolutely. Congratulations, Matt," Mona said.

"That's great, dude." Jace grinned.

"It's all because of you. All the pointers you gave me and how much you made me practice. Oh, man. Thanks, Jace."

"I didn't really do anything, but you are entirely welcome for whatever you think I did. I'm proud of you, Matt."

"I wish you could come to the game. It's this Friday—" he shrugged his shoulders "—but I know you probably can't." Matt turned to Kelly. "Cory is picking me up in a few minutes. He's the quarterback. We're gonna grab a burger and talk about some plays. I'll be home before ten," he added before bounding from the room.

"Do you have any plans for Friday evening?"

Her gaze shot to Jace in surprise. She shrugged. "Not that I know of."

"Want to go to a football game?" He was grinning from ear to ear.

"Matt's?"

"Yeah."

"I would love to go."

Matt's first varsity game. It would be doubly special to share it with Jace. The thought of being seen in public with him made her a bit nervous, but Matt had mentioned that most everyone in town knew Jace Compton was living among them. After the media reports that had lasted for weeks, the world probably knew. And apparently, Matt hadn't hidden the fact that he and his sister lived on the ranch. And really, why would he? So it was pointless for them to attend the game separately.

"I'll meet you in the kitchen. About six thirty?"

"Jace, what about you going out in public?"

He shrugged those broad shoulders. "I have no intention of living my life in hiding. Tom says it has been quiet for a couple of weeks. The folks of this community seem like good people. I really want to see Matt's game."

Kelly assured herself the inner excitement she felt was the anticipation over seeing Matt play, but she knew part of it was about going with Jace. As his date. It would be the first time they'd gone out together since he'd moved to this ranch.

As she counted down the days Kelly had to wonder what the news media might do if they saw her and Jace out and about together. All she could do was put her trust in Jace and hope that he knew what he was doing.

By six thirty on Friday, Kelly had joined Jace in the kitchen and soon they were on their way to the stadium, followed by two bodyguards in a separate vehicle.

The snare drums of the local band beat out a cadence, adding to the spirit and excitement in the air as the small entourage reached the front of the old wooden bleachers. They climbed the steps, heading to a spot that would give them a better view of the field and hopefully allow Jace some degree of anonymity. He didn't seem worried about it. His small two-person detachment would ensure his safety, handling any situation should it get out of hand. The two men were dressed in jeans and T-shirts with light jackets helping to camouflage the weapons they no doubt carried underneath; one of them led the way while the other brought up the rear.

"Fall is on its way," Kelly said as she sat down next to Jace.

"Are you cold?"

She shook her head. "No. It's a perfect temperature. I'm just glad we're past the worst of the Texas summer heat. You'll learn to appreciate November weather."

He laughed. "Be glad Matt isn't playing football in the northeast. I've been on the field when you couldn't see the yard lines for the snow. Played during a blizzard one year."

"How is that possible? How can anyone play in a blizzard?"

"The best way you can." He grinned.

"You loved it, didn't you?" She could see it in his eyes. Regardless of anything else Jace had accomplished in his life, his true love was football.

He nodded, his gaze on the field. "Yeah. I loved every

second," he said, and then turned to Kelly. The dark glitter of his eyes took her breath away. "It was the second best time of my life."

She smiled, immediately understanding his implication. The urge to lean toward him and taste those wickedly handsome lips was overwhelming.

The band began a rousing school fight song and everyone sprang to their feet, clapping and cheering as the home team broke through the colorful paper barrier and jogged onto the field. The black-and-gold uniforms of the Calico Springs Cougars stood out against the bright green turf. It was high school sports at its best. Jace, Kelly and the security team stood and cheered along with the other three hundred people in attendance.

It was surreal, being at a game in the town where she'd grown up, watching her kid brother among the varsity players, while standing next to Jace. The stadium lights made the colors more vivid; the air was thick with excitement. As they tossed the coin and the kickoff ensued, Kelly watched with pride as Matt took his place in the starting lineup.

As the game progressed, becoming more intense, Jace whistled and shouted his encouragement. When the Cougars made the first touchdown of the night, he pulled Kelly into his strong arms and hugged her in a tight embrace.

During halftime, Kelly noticed people walking below them as they made their way back and forth between the refreshment booth and their seats. They would look up at Jace and wave. If he saw them, Jace waved back, displaying that sparkling smile. Only a few approached, welcoming him to their community, wanting only to shake his hand. Their courtesy made Kelly feel a pride for her hometown she'd never really felt before.

"Would you like anything? Soft drink, coffee, hot dog?"

"No, thanks, I'm fine."

Her gaze wandered over his handsomely cut features, lingering for an instant on the strong line of his mouth. She couldn't stop herself from remembering how his kisses had so easily destroyed her preconceived notions of just how erotic a kiss could be. She'd way underestimated the power of a kiss. At least where Jace was concerned.

More than a little unnerved by the intensity of his glance, she forced her gaze back to the field with a shuddering breath.

By the third quarter, the score was tied. The Vikings had the ball. Their quarterback threw a pass and all eyes were on the ball as it soared through the air. At the last instant, it was intercepted. By Matt. Jace was on his feet, with Kelly close behind him. The crowd roared as Matt darted and circled in and around his opponents, jumping free of hands that would take him down. The spectators were on their feet as Matt ran down the length of the field toward the goal post, making it to the thirty yard line before he was finally tackled. Kelly was ecstatic. She swallowed past a lump in her throat as she clenched her hands together, overwhelmed with pride.

Jace caught her gaze and grinned at her reaction. He clearly shared in the pride she felt for her brother. With his run downfield, Matt had set his team up for an easy touchdown. He was the hero of the night.

When there were only three minutes remaining on the clock, Jace's security encouraged them to leave. With the home team ahead by two touchdowns, Jace hesitantly agreed.

"Do you mind?"

"Not at all. I think it's a good idea. Matt will understand. He's been talking all week about a postgame party at the pizza place. They'll no doubt rehash every second of the game. He's going to be floating on cloud nine for a month."

"He has every right to." Jace offered her his hand as he stood up, and she took it. "He did great. He still has this year plus two more to expand his knowledge and hone his skills before college. And he's a natural. He's got a chance at the pros, barring any injury, if that's what he wants."

"I wish Gramps could be here. But I'm grateful Matt has you. Thank you for all you've done for him, Jace."

He shrugged his shoulders. "It was my pleasure, whatever you think I did. Giving Matt some tips wasn't the reason for his accomplishments tonight. He did that all on his own."

As they walked out to the parking lot, she reflected on how she'd seen another facet of Jace Compton tonight. And she had to admit, she liked what she saw.

The drive back to the ranch was quiet, but it was an easy silence. Jace pulled into the main entrance and walked with Kelly through the trees to her cabin.

"I enjoyed it, Jace. Very much," she said as they went inside.

"So did I."

"I guess I'll see you tomorrow."

"Yeah. Tomorrow." For a few seconds their gazes locked across the darkened room.

Reaching out to her, Jace cupped her face, drawing her closer. Lowering his head, he gently kissed her, loving the softness of her lips, the taste of her. Her purely feminine essence called out to him and his body tensed in readiness.

He was about to pull away when she opened her lips to him. His heartbeat quickened and he deepened the kiss. His arms came around her, pulling her tightly to him; he loved the way her smaller body molded perfectly to his. He cupped the back of her head, his fingers lost in the silky texture of her hair. Raw need surged through his body, demanding he hold her close, ensuring she wouldn't turn away.

She was beyond tempting. The need to feel her underneath him once again, taking the pleasure he gave and giving it back ten times over, was eating him up inside. Kelly was everything he'd ever wanted in a woman. He never wanted to let her go.

But he knew it was wrong. She didn't need an affair. She needed a husband and a permanent home. He couldn't offer her either one.

Kelly moaned softly and Jace struggled to keep his passion under control. As the fragrance of her perfume blended with the scent of her desire and the sweet taste of her lips, he knew he was going to lose this battle.

The sound of the latch on the front door being turned and the door opening helped bring Jace to his senses. With more strength than he thought he possessed, he lifted his lips from hers and glanced toward the door.

Matt and two of his buddies stood in the doorway, grinning as if they'd just found gold.

"Oops. Gosh I'm sorry," Matt ventured, but didn't look sorry at all. "Forgot my wallet." He walked over to the kitchen counter and grabbed the dark leather billfold. Returning to the door, he glanced back at Jace, and then looked directly at his sister. "Click. Click." And with a chuckle, they were gone.

"Click. Click?"

"Don't ask," Kelly returned, shaking her head.

A sexy grin kicked up the corners of his mouth. "Your brother isn't sixteen. He's sixteen going on forty."

He reached out and pushed the sweater from her shoulders, and then removed the band holding back her hair. He grabbed the front of her jeans and pulled her closer, unfastening and unzipping.

"This isn't going to resolve anything," she whispered against his mouth. "But I'm tired of telling you no."

His heart rate tripled. "Then don't."

He was on fire. He didn't know how they were going to contend with the future, but at the moment, it didn't matter. It was enough to know she wanted him. As if to make sure he knew, she kissed him with a hunger he remembered so well, her hands fisting his shirt, leaving no doubt in his mind they were going to make love. He was going to take her. Right here. Right now. He was delirious with need. His blood pounded in his ears and he let out a deep growl.

Kelly was his.

He backed her against the cabin wall and kissed her, over and over, long and deep, his tongue caressing hers, making a silent demand that had her clinging to him.

He grabbed the hem of her T-shirt and quickly pulled it over her head. He took off her bra next, and sucked first one breast, then the other, while his hand alternately massaged and teased.

She began unbuttoning his shirt, but with one hard tug, Jace ripped it open, buttons flying everywhere. Her hands roamed over the smooth skin of his muscular chest, and then he felt her lips and tongue against him as she tasted him. As though she could never get enough.

He lowered one hand to between her legs. Even through her jeans, he felt the intense heat. The dampness. The scent of her desire surrounded him. She pushed against his hand and he heard a small whimper.

Without another word, Jace scooped her into his arms and carried her to the bedroom that wasn't full of sports equipment, closing the door behind him. He placed her on the soft mattress, shrugged out of his shirt and kicked off his boots. He quickly removed her jeans and then dropped his own.

The vision in front of him stole his breath. Her long blond hair draped over the pillow, her perfect breasts full and swollen, the light pink tips now hard nubs. But it was the sleepy, steamy look of want in her eyes that held him transfixed, the awareness and need clearly displayed in those blue-green eyes. Her lips, slightly open, showing brilliant white teeth, enticed him even further.

He placed one knee on the side of the bed, bending over her, his face stopping a breath away from hers. He cupped her chin, his thumb rubbing over her lower lip. Her lips closed around him and she moaned. He felt her teeth as she bit down, teasing him, sucking him deeper inside.

With a moan, he took her in a long, deep kiss. He moved to bite at her jaw, and then trailed kisses along her neck, licking, tasting, loving her down to her breasts. When he drew the hard peak of one breast into his mouth, her body surged toward his and she whimpered. He caressed the other breast in his hand, teasing, molding her. His erection throbbed with need to be inside her.

"Kelly," he growled. He could hear the animal rawness in his own voice. Using one hand, he positioned himself and pushed inside her. He stopped to allow her body time to adjust and accept his girth, and then filled her with one hard thrust. The heat and silkiness of her body was more amazing than he remembered. Hands cupping her hips, he held her up to him and filled her again and again. She called out his name as the pace became faster. Hotter. Frantic. He felt her shatter, her release pushing him over the top and beyond. It seemed to go on forever, yet it was too brief. Gasping for air, Jace dropped to his side, pulling her close, bestowing kisses on her face, her hair.

For long moments Jace held her in the darkness, her head resting on his chest, her spicy fragrance filling the air around him. Kelly was his. Every cell in his body screamed it.

There had to be a way for them to be together. He had to find a way.

He must have fallen asleep, because when he opened his eyes, there was faint sunlight coming in through the window. The sun was barely creeping over the far horizon when he awoke. Kelly was still in his arms, her head on his chest and one arm resting across his abdomen. He kissed the top of her head, his hands playing in the long tendrils of her hair. She stretched, raised her head and opened her eyes. The gleam in those blue-green depths was mesmerizing.

"Good morning," he whispered. "Sleep well?"

"Yes." She smiled up at him. The satisfaction of their night's lovemaking clearly shone on her face. "And you?"

"I'm still dreaming." He cupped her face, pressing a soft kiss on her lips. "What time will Matt be home?"

"Noon."

"Good. Because this was billed as a double feature and I'm pretty sure it's rated triple X."

She grinned before his mouth covered hers, and once again he was lost in the magic that was Kelly.

Thirteen

By the time Kelly made it upstairs to her office on Monday, the phones were already ringing off the hook. Kelly settled the baby in the crib and hurried to her desk. The day turned fast and furious and before she knew it, Mona was calling it to an end.

At the end of this week they would all fly to Los Angeles for Mona's charity gala. Then Jace would stay in town for a series of meetings on his next film project. Kelly and Mona would return to the ranch.

On Tuesday, Jace stopped by Mona's office. Her heart went into double time, but he only asked how her weekend had been and wished both Kelly and his mom a good day. He seemed to be giving Kelly space to sort it all out, to come to grips with their renewed love affair.

He couldn't know she already had.

Downstairs that afternoon she found Jace sitting in the kitchen on one of the bar stools, an inch of printed pages in a thick blue binder open on the counter in front of him.

Jace glanced up. "You leaving for the day?"

"Yep." She switched Henry from one arm to the other. "Is that your script?"

"Yeah." Jace glanced down at the papers. "I need to read the damn thing but I'm having a hard time concentrating. Thought maybe sitting out here would help."

He pushed the script aside and reached out to touch Henry's foot. "He's growing."

"Yes, he is."

"Are you and Mom almost ready for her charity event?" he asked before she could turn away.

"I think we're right on schedule. If as many people come as have responded so far, there'll be over four hundred in attendance. Mona is ecstatic."

Jace grinned. "What about you? Are you looking forward to it?"

"*Me?* I'll enjoy seeing it all come together, but I'm not attending the actual dinner and ball."

Jace frowned. "Why not?"

"Because."

"Can you elaborate just a bit?"

"I'm an employee." Her tone said he was dumb for asking. "Mona will have a full catering staff to assist her with drinks and hors d'oeuvres. The food will be prepared on site, overseen by the chef who has assisted Mona at the ball for the past five years. I'll be there to help set up, make sure everything is going according to plan, but once the guests start arriving I'll stay in the background as a precautionary measure. Basically, by then, my job will be over."

"Does Mom know your plans?"

"We talked." She hoped Jace didn't try to muddy the water. It had taken her quite a while to convince Mona she did not want or need to be there during the actual festivities. The social class of the guests was intimidating… Senators. Congressmen. Award-winning actors and producers. The elite of the elite. Kelly didn't need to be reminded she was about as far away from their inner circles as a person could get. And she had no intention of subjecting herself or Mona to any embarrassment she might cause if she committed a faux pas at the gala.

And there was the expense of a gown. No way was she spending a thousand dollars or more on something she would wear only once. She had a hard enough time making herself buy a brand of green beans that wasn't on sale. Her frugal nature didn't allow for thousand-dollar dresses. Being a guest at Mona's ball was simply not going to happen.

"Your mom and I have it all worked out, Jace," she said with as much happy bravado as she could muster. "No worries."

No worries.

With Kelly, that usually meant there was definitely something to worry about. Jace picked up the script as she walked out of the room, heading for the back door. With a frown, he rolled the document up in his hand and headed to his mother's bedroom.

"Mom?"

"Come in, sweetheart." Mona smiled as she entered the bedroom from the adjacent powder room. "I think I may have forgotten something regarding the ball. I just can't remember what it is." She chuckled. "Do you think that really does mean it isn't important?"

Jace shook his head. "I'm afraid I couldn't help you with that one, Mother. Change of subject. I just talked to Kelly downstairs and she said she's not attending the charity event. I thought you both were going. You both went through the dress fitting."

"Yes, I know." His mother sighed. "And she balked at the idea even then. She says she'd be out of her league around the people we expect to be there. Her words, not mine. She contends she's only an employee and has no business going."

"They're not one damn bit better than she is."

"I know, Jace."

He muttered an angry curse under his breath. "Give it another try, will you, Mom?"

"Tomorrow," she promised.

Jace said good-night and headed to his room, his molars grinding in frustration. Kelly shouldn't be concerned about a bunch of blowhard politicians and a few egotistical actors. He'd counted on her being there. He wasn't sure why, other than that she and Matt had become part of the family. Kelly wasn't an employee. He awoke every morning looking forward to seeing her and the baby. For reasons he didn't understand, Kelly's presence calmed him. As infuriating as she could be at times, Jace would take the frustrating with the good anytime. Her being in his life was…right. He was the one who was wrong for her.

Other than dealing with the constant, overwhelming need to make love to her, his life was good. Clearly he should have said something to her about the charity event and asked if she would be his date. Was he ever going to get it right?

"You know, we must go shopping," Mona stated the next day as she and Kelly ate lunch in the kitchen.

"For what?" She crumbled crackers into her bowl of soup.

"For the charity ball."

Kelly wasn't sure she understood. Everything had been ordered down to the last flower. "Have I missed something?" She put down her spoon, mentally going over the details of the plans for the event. "They called and confirmed they would have the ice sculpture delivered by four on the day of the ball. The chef has said—"

"The preparations are fine. You've done an outstanding job. I was referring to us. Surely you know I expect you to attend the gala."

"Yes. No. I mean yes, I know I'll be going but not as a guest. I'll work behind the scenes, stick to the kitchen area. I'll be at the hotel Saturday afternoon to help oversee everything, but like I said before, I have no business attending the ball."

Mona looked at Kelly as if she'd grown a second head. "And why not?"

The idea was so ridiculous. She didn't want to offend this kind, wonderful woman, but going to an event attended by some of the biggest names in both Hollywood and politics was not going to happen. Talk about feeling like a fish out of water.

Kelly just shook her head, refusing to discuss it further, but Mona wasn't going to let it drop.

"You listen to me, Kelly Michaels. This isn't one of Jace's red carpet extravaganzas. It's my charity ball. And as my personal assistant, you are most certainly expected to attend. And you will need a gown to wear, unless you have one already?"

Kelly closed her eyes in temporary defeat and shook her head.

"No? Then Andre will provide the gowns as I originally intended. I'll call him myself and reconfirm."

What had she gotten herself into? She was not part of their world. It was just wrong to think differently. Of course, she wanted to be there for Mona. No matter how carefully one planned, there were always last-minute details to see to. But to attend the gala dressed as one of the guests was just wrong.

The trip to Los Angeles in Jace's Gulfstream was smooth and filled with laughter as Mona recalled mishaps from her past charity events. Kelly enjoyed listening to the banter but the uneasiness hadn't left her. She should not be attending this elite event. And no amount of winks from Jace or pats on the hand from Mona was going to change that.

Arriving at the hotel the day before the event, they hit the ground running. Kelly quickly realized that when Mona Compton set her mind to do something, anyone not going in her direction had better get out of the way. This fundraiser was her passion.

Kelly did her best to keep up, but lack of experience initially left her feeling completely out of her depth. Thankfully, the hotel staff had been prepped and things were accomplished efficiently and to Mona's liking. Kelly oversaw the setup of the banquet hall. The tables, chairs and decorations were brought through the door as fast as she could place them. Meanwhile Mona met with the chef and culinary artists who would provide the special touches that made this occasion a Mona Compton event.

"I think we're done," Mona said the next day as she looked around at the vast ballroom. "The ice sculpture will be delivered at four. Where should it go?"

"I thought we'd put it in an area near the dessert buffet but with enough space in between to make it accessible on all sides." Kelly walked over to the spot. "Around here. There is even an electrical outlet. We can use fluorescent lighting to make it the focus without melting it too badly."

"Perfect. I need to make a couple of changes to the place cards, only because I know these people." She rolled her eyes. "Sometimes it's better to avoid a potentially unpleasant situation than it is to cross your fingers and hope nothing will happen. You'll learn soon enough." She laughed. "Take this card and switch it for any one on the table over there in the corner." After five additional changes, Mona deemed the seating arrangement done.

"Okay," Mona said, "now it's time for us to get ready." She glanced at her watch. "Your dress should be in your room. Let's head to the salon for hair and make-up first."

"Hair? Make-up?"

"Why, of course, dear."

Of course.

Two hours later, Kelly stepped inside her room. Immediately, she saw a large bouquet on the table next to the windows. Tossing her clipboard onto the bed, she approached the flowers. There were several different varieties and the fragrance was amazing. Kelly opened the card.

To my dearest Kelly. I couldn't have done this without you. Mona.

Kelly sat down on the striped silk-covered chair nearest the small table. With all she had to do, Mona had taken the time and the trouble to send her a beautiful and thoughtful thank-you.

Tears welled in her eyes and she fought to keep them from spilling over. This was all happening because of Jace. It was because of him she was here now. It was because of him she had a great job working for an amazing lady.

She placed a quick call to Mrs. Jenkins to check on Henry, receiving the assurance the baby was fine. Then Kelly turned toward the closet.

She unzipped the black garment bag containing her dress for the gala, refusing to speculate on how much it cost.

Her eyes grew wide. Her mouth dropped open. This couldn't be right. Removing the gown from the closet, she held it up. This wasn't the design she'd expected. Not even close. Someone had made a terrible mistake. The dress was not blue. It wasn't satin. It was exquisite black lace, from top to bottom.

A few minutes later she stood in front of the mirror, her reflection nothing like what she was used to seeing. Not by a mile. The stylist had pulled her long hair to one side, the ends curled into ringlets that fell over her shoulder and down her back. The long-sleeved black lace gown fell to her feet, with a short train at the back. The form-fitting dress highlighted every curve.

It was expensive. It was elegant. It was risqué.

It was so not her.

She couldn't go downstairs in this.

She glanced at the clock. Seven fifteen. The event started at eight. A full panic attack hit her with the velocity of an air bag deployed during an unexpected crash. Placing her hands against her temples, Kelly tried to calm her racing heart enough to think. *What was she going to do?* How could she hurt Mona by not showing up for the festivities? How could she refuse to wear a gown that must have cost thousands of dollars? Yet she couldn't wear this in front of all those people. They would stare. She would die. What had the designer been thinking? He obviously sent the wrong dress. She'd expected something like a blue prom dress and instead received an elegant black spiderweb.

Clearly, she shouldn't have let Mona and the designer make the selection. She'd just blown it off the day the man came to the ranch to take fittings. When asked if she wanted to look at styles, she'd politely refused, thinking she wouldn't be going anyway so it wouldn't matter. She couldn't have imagined that with that small action, she'd pulled the trigger and shot herself in the foot.

Fourteen

"Have you seen Kelly?" Jace asked his mom as he scanned the people entering the ballroom.

"No. I haven't seen her since we had our hair done this afternoon and... Oh dear."

"Oh dear?" Jace eyed his mother. "What?"

His mother suddenly appeared apprehensive. "You may need to go up and encourage her to come down."

"Why? I mean, I'll be glad to, but I thought it was settled that she would attend."

"It is. It was. She, uh...she might not be completely happy with her gown."

Jace frowned. "Why would you say that?"

"Oh dear. Jason, please go up to her room and see if you can talk to her. She left the dress selection up to me and I may have made the wrong decision."

His mother wrung her hands, obvious concern in every feature of her face.

What in the world did his mother consider *the wrong decision*?

He rushed up to Kelly's suite. After two raps on the door, she immediately pulled it open. Quickly she looked past him down the long hall, first one way then the other. Grabbing his arm, she yanked him inside, shutting the door behind them.

There were no words for the vision standing before him. Jace swallowed hard. His body surged to readiness. Kelly was a natural beauty, but in that dress, every man at the ball would beat a fast path straight to her. His protective instinct jumped to the fore.

"You look…incredibly beautiful."

She pushed away from the door and walked past him into the suite, her hands fidgeting at her sides. Apparently, she felt something was terribly wrong. The only thing *he* felt wrong was that a certain part of his anatomy was about to explode.

"I can't do this," she said. "I can't go downstairs."

"Why not?" He frowned.

"You're kidding, right? Wearing *this*?"

"What do you think is wrong with it?"

"There isn't enough material to make a shirt for Henry."

"Kelly, you're way overreacting."

"I am not. Oh God. Jace, you've got to help me. I can't hurt your mother."

"Why can't you go in the dress? It's amazing. You look… ravishing. Good enough to eat."

"I'm serious."

"So am I."

"Look at it."

"Believe me, I am."

"It makes me look as if I'm not wearing anything but a few scanty strips of lace."

"And you think that's a bad thing?"

"Well, it isn't *good*."

Jace ran his hand over the lower part of his face. He didn't know what to say. Kelly was beyond gorgeous and sexy and that dress just confirmed it. She would be the sensation of the ball. How could she not realize how beautiful she looked? Had she looked in a mirror?

"The dress is fine. It's beyond fine. And we need to go. Dinner will be called in about thirty minutes. We'll need to find our seats."

Her hands began to fidget again. "Maybe I'll go down later. Food is the last thing I want right now. Anyway, there's no place card for me at the any of the tables. I made sure of it. I'm only an employee, Jace, playing dress-up for the night. And your date won't appreciate it at all if you show up with me on your arm."

"I'm looking at my date for the evening."

"You... I... No. You can't."

"Why not?"

"You *know*. Anyway, I'm not ready."

"You look more than ready to me. And I assure you, there is a place card at the table, next to me. You're good. Mom's better. You look beautiful. Now get anything you want to take with you and let's go before I lock the door and help you out of the dress you don't like."

"Jace, *please*." She moved farther inside the room. "There will be reporters. It will look bad for Mona if you walk into the room with me. The gold digger from Texas."

"Kelly, tonight you're my date," he stated, stepping toward her. "A very beautiful date. In that dress, every man here will sit up and take notice."

"I feel like a sideshow freak. Did you have a stripper pole put in the ballroom?"

He inhaled deeply and rubbed the back of his neck. He knew women who didn't give full nudity a second thought. Kelly was still an innocent in so many ways. It was part of the charm he found so irresistible. He understood after the media blitz about the baby that she was also trying to protect Mona and the charity. She couldn't be more wrong. But he didn't have time for the argument she would no doubt wage. He looked from Kelly through the open door to the large bed in the room to his left.

"If you really don't want to go downstairs, I can't make you." He'd make damn sure the locks were set.

"Oh," Kelly inhaled a deep sigh of relief. "Thank you, Jace."

He slipped out of his jacket, tossed it onto a chair and

then pulled at the end of his bow tie, pulling it free from its knot.

"What are you doing?"

"If you don't go, I don't go." He walked into the bedroom and pulled back the covers on the bed. "I'll just stay here with you. I'm betting we can find something to do."

"You can't do that to Mona." Then she straightened as the light dawned about what he was doing. "This is blackmail."

He shrugged. "As they say, all's fair. Which is it going to be, Kelly? Are you going to accompany me downstairs or do we get out of these clothes and spend the night together in that bed like we both really want to do?"

"Don't do this, Jace."

"I haven't done anything. Yet."

"Jace."

He walked up to her and cupped her face in his hands. If he didn't get them out of this room fast, neither of them would ever make it to the ballroom. His mother might be a little pissed, but he was past the point of caring.

"Take me very seriously, Kelly." His eyes held her gaze. "There's nothing I want to do right now more than remove that dress, inch by inch, and carry you to the bed." He took her hand and pressed her palm against his throbbing erection. "You need to decide. Now."

As soon as they stepped off the elevators, they were surrounded. People filled every available space, in the corridor, around the elevators, in the ballroom, even filling the elegant hotel lobby. As soon as Jace was spotted, reporters came out of the woodwork. Cameras flashed while reporters stood in line for an interview. Jace held Kelly's hand, refusing to let her fade into the background. He gave interview after interview focusing on the charity. He noted his mom across the room doing the same thing. Kelly stood quietly at his side until some of the questions were directed at her.

"Ms. Michaels, are you excited about this charity ball tonight?"

"Of course." She looked into the camera, a beautiful smile on her lips. "We're all excited to be a part of this very worthy cause."

"What about the man standing next to you? Any wedding bells in the near future?"

Before Jace could open his mouth, Kelly responded to the question. "We're here tonight to raise money to help women who are abused and desperate to find a better life for themselves and their children. It's a serious concern and I would expect the media to respect that and focus on the women who so desperately need our help."

"So you're refusing to comment on any personal relationship between yourself and Jace Compton?"

"Yes. As a matter of fact, I am. This is neither the time nor the place for questions of that nature. Now, if you're willing to hand me a check for a million dollars made out to the NCAW, I might be tempted to answer."

Jace was stunned by just how easily Kelly shut the man down. It was as though she had years of experience in front of the reporters' cameras. The poor guy never had a chance. He mumbled something about not having quite that much in his pocket, the others laughed, and further questions along those lines were dropped. Jace had never been prouder of anyone in his life. Though her body trembled the entire time, she'd handled it like a pro.

After dinner, the orchestra began playing. Couples rose from their seats and headed for the dance floor. Jace stood, placed his linen napkin on the table, and held out his hand to Kelly. She gracefully accepted.

He pulled her close, taking advantage of the opportunity to have her next to him. It felt so right.

"Remember when we danced in that little hotel lounge in Calico Springs?" he murmured near her ear. "It was dark. The only light was from the candles on the tables. I could have held you like that forever. And we still fit together perfectly."

"Only because you're a great dancer."

"Dancing has nothing to do with how impeccably you fit in my arms. If you like, I can demonstrate other ways we fit together."

"Be nice."

"I'm trying. But all I seem to want to do is be naughty. Very, very naughty."

"I don't know whether to laugh or take you seriously and issue a reprimand."

"Serious works for me." He leaned down and whispered in her ear, "You can even spank me if you want."

"Jace!" He loved the delicate blush that covered her fine features.

"What?" He intentionally assumed a look of pure innocence. Then couldn't hold back the grin at the expression of reproach on her face.

"You are bad."

"Mmmm. That's not what you said a week ago."

"May I cut in?" asked a man standing next to Jace, his eyes all over Kelly.

Jace nodded and pulled a gulp of air through his nose, aware he couldn't say no.

He watched helplessly as the man stepped up and put his arms around Kelly. She gave Jace a strained smile before they disappeared into the crowd.

"Well, hello there, handsome."

Jace turned to find Lena Maxwell, her dark auburn hair soft and wispy around her bare shoulders.

"Lena. How are you?" His eyes darted from Lena to the crowd on the dance floor as he tried to keep Kelly in sight. "Thanks for coming tonight."

"The pleasure is all mine." The sultry actress gave a deep-throated laugh. "Now dance with me before I have to take another breath without your arms around me."

With a tight smile, Jace complied.

"I heard you bought a ranch. Surely you're not retiring from pictures?"

"Haven't decided. Just knew I needed a break. What about you? Still fending off the offers with a stick?"

She laughed again. Jace searched the room for Kelly.

"She got to you big-time, didn't she?"

"Who?"

"The little blonde on your arm tonight. Congratulations on fatherhood, by the way."

"Thanks." Lena was trying to dig for gossip. She loved the spotlight, and knowing something no one else knew kept her right where she wanted to be.

"Brilliant idea to bring her here tonight. It will be all over the front page by in the morning. Good for the charity. Great for your career at the same time. Rumors are going to fly. Your name will be bandied about for weeks." She gave a sultry laugh. "Now I understand why we haven't seen you for a while."

Jace clenched his teeth in an effort to keep his temper at bay. Lena was the perfect example of why Kelly had been so concerned about attending tonight. He only hoped she wouldn't see this as a setup and think he was using her exactly as Lena described.

"May I cut in?" Another woman was waiting patiently by their side.

"So much for keeping you all to myself," Lena muttered, but politely stepped away. With a quick wink at Jace she disappeared toward the refreshment bar.

"Still have to stand in line to get to the great Jace Compton." The pretty brunette stepped into his arms. "Some things will never change."

"How've you been, Audrey?"

Jace absently moved to the music, only partially listening to the woman's ongoing chatter. He'd attended dozens of these affairs but tonight, for the first time, he saw nothing even remotely enjoyable in the experience. He didn't want to make small talk. He didn't want to be on center stage. Suddenly all the phony flirting and keeping up a front turned his stomach.

He wanted the quiet of the ranch and the privacy it offered. And right or wrong, he wanted Kelly beside him.

The next man who stepped on her foot was going to regret it, Kelly decided as yet another intoxicated, overbearing fool asked her to dance. What was with the hands? This was an upscale event to raise money for a very worthy cause, not some grab-'n'-go on the shady side of town—even if she was half-naked. The cowhands had better manners.

Mona had called it right. There had to be at least four hundred people crowded into the ballroom. More than half were men, and she speculated that the majority of those were either blitzed or well on their way.

She'd spotted Jace a couple of times, each time trying to sidestep a different woman. They flirted shamelessly with him. He smiled politely but didn't appear to encourage them. He looked extraordinarily handsome in a tuxedo. At one point, their eyes met. He didn't smile, but the look that flared in his eyes warmed her down to her toes.

When the song ended, Kelly took the opportunity to excuse herself and leave the dance floor. She made her way to the ladies' room, hoping the evening would soon end. While it wasn't as bad as she'd first imagined, her feet were aching and her facial muscles actually hurt from continuously smiling, something she'd never before experienced. Perhaps it wasn't too late to call Mrs. Jenkins and again check on Henry.

She entered the elegant powder room, passing through to get to the bathroom facilities. As she was getting ready to exit, she heard the voices of several women in the first room.

"So...what did you think of Jace's new *friend*?"

Several giggles were the reply.

"I think she's nice," one of the women said.

"Oh, honey. She is going to be his downfall. I can't believe she managed to get pregnant. My husband said Jace was not enthusiastic at all about the new film. I guarantee it's because he feels responsible for that woman and her baby."

"Surely he won't turn down the role?" another woman asked. "I heard he is going to be offered the lead."

"She will probably *let* him do it. As long as it puts more money in her bank account."

What? Grabbing the handle, Kelly wrenched open the restroom door and turned toward the women in the powder room. She'd put up with that gossipy bullshit in school. All the talk about her father. Accusing *her* of breaking up marriages. She'd be damned if she would quietly take the hits again or hide like some thief in the night and say nothing as she had before.

"Frankly, I doubt she cares one way or the other. Would you? I mean, she's got her hooks in the most eligible bachelor on this continent. But she'd better ask herself how long she can keep him toeing the line."

"Maybe we should ask her for some pointers."

"Yeah. Maybe you should," Kelly interjected, staring at the speaker and wishing her gaze could do serious damage. "It certainly couldn't hurt." She let her gaze slide from the woman's face down to her feet and back, keeping a look of disgust on her face. "But it absolutely won't help. Excuse me."

Kelly pushed her way through the little group and looked into the large floor-to-ceiling mirror. Puckering her lips, she pretended to check her lipstick and then turned her head from side to side, her hand brushing down the side of her face and neck as if looking for flaws before shrugging her shoulders as though not finding any. Turning to look at herself in profile, she sucked in her stomach, arched her back and stuck out her boobs. What little she had.

"Mmm." She muttered in a disgruntled moan. She ran her hand over her stomach then across her breasts. "There's just too much material to this dress. Don't you think?"

The three women stared, each presenting a different level of shock, resentment and indignation.

"Oh well. I guess I'll leave that up to Jacie. Maybe he likes taking it off better." *Fake smile.* "You girls know what I mean." *Fade to frown.* "Oh. Or maybe you don't." *Uncaring shrug.* "Pity."

"Don't you live on a *farm*?"

One of the women, the oldest, apparently decided she had what it took to bring Kelly down a peg or two. *Bring it on, bitch.* These women were nothing compared to the kids at Calico Springs High.

Pointing finger. Surprised tone. "You're Celesta Mason!" *Aha look.* "I *thought* I recognized you." *Big smile.* "*Your* husband is the one who was caught humping one of the cooks in the kitchen two years ago. Naughty, naughty boy. But then..." *Conspiratorial tone.* "...can anyone really blame him?"

The gasps from all three could have sucked the plaster off the walls. Thank God for Mona's idle chitchat while they were placing the name cards earlier today. With a last glare in Kelly's direction, Celesta stomped toward the door, her face getting redder with each step. Her friends followed close behind.

"Bye-bye," Kelly called in her sweetest voice before the heavy door closed. *And good riddance.* She was gaining a much clearer picture of the way this game was played. Take away the million-dollar entitlements and these people were no different from the wannabes in Calico Springs.

She walked out of the ladies' room intending to check in with Mona and return to her suite. Her feet were killing her. Four hours in five-inch heels was not her thing. Before she could take three steps, she felt an arm slip around her shoulders.

"I was afraid I'd missed you, sweetheart." A man she didn't know smiled down at her. "I've waited long enough. Let's dance."

Oh, brother. He took her hand and pulled her into the ballroom, holding her far too close. He reeked of alcohol. His eyes looked cloudy; his pupils were dilated, making her wonder if he was high on booze or drugs. Probably both. He leaned forward, placing a kiss on her shoulder.

"Don't." Kelly was beyond disgusted. She'd had enough.

"You staying here at the hotel?"

She ignored his question, trying to think of a way out of this situation without making a scene.

"Come on, baby," he persisted, "what say you and me get out of here? I can think of a lot better things to do."

"I don't think so." She tried to push away, but he held her firmly in his arms.

"Don't be a fool." His voice suddenly sounded malicious. "If you think you and your kid are enough to make Jace leave the industry, you're sadly mistaken." He laughed harshly. "Yeah, I saw the way you looked at him across the room. But he's too into Lena Maxwell to care about anyone else. It's been that way for years. If you're smart, you'll let it go."

"You seem to know an awful lot about Jace Compton."

"We go way back. Sorry babe, maybe I should have introduced myself. Most people know me on sight. I'm Bret Goldman."

Bret Goldman. The man she'd spoken to when she'd called to tell Jace about the baby. So this was the jackass in person.

"It's okay, sweetheart. You're new. You'll learn."

"What will I learn?" She pushed back from him enough to look at his face. He was handsome enough, but his arrogance overshadowed any attraction someone might feel. Plus, he had some serious graying at the temples, and he carried the general look of one who overindulged. In everything, apparently.

"Who to be nice to and who doesn't matter. I matter."

"Really? To whom?"

His eyes narrowed. She needed to get away from this guy. Making a scene was becoming less and less important. Elite gala or not, he was about to be on the receiving end of an easily understood no.

He laughed contemptuously. "Be very careful, honey. Some people you don't say no to. I'm one of them."

Kelly could only gape at his arrogance. She tried her best to stifle a laugh, but the giggle broke free in an uncontainable snort. Suffice it to say it did not go over well with Mr. Full-of-Himself.

The man glared and seized her wrist. "Let's see if I can give you a better understanding upstairs." He began to pull her out of the room toward the elevators. The conceited jerk was serious. This had gone too far.

"Remove your hand. Now."

"A little wildcat. I love it."

"I don't think Ms. Michaels wants to party, Bret."

Bret stopped and Kelly looked behind her into Jace's strong face. He was clearly holding his anger in check. To someone passing it would appear they were all just having a nice conversation. But Jace had a deadly look in his beautiful green eyes. Anyone with any common sense at all would know to back off. Immediately.

"She's a little tease. We'll get past that upstairs."

Kelly struggled to remember...was she stronger with her left knee or her right?

"Let her go, Bret."

"Or what?" the man challenged.

There were no more words as Jace's fist shot out, landing squarely against the man's nose with a force that would have made Rocky Balboa proud. Bret released her arm as he crashed to the floor, taking out a waiter carrying a tray full of dirty plates in the process.

With a few muttered curses, Bret got to his feet. He

brushed at the trickle of blood running from his nose and the sight of it seemed to set him off. He lunged at Jace and grabbed his arm and swung him around, his fist flying toward Jace's face. With a quick, easy move, Jace avoided any contact and sent the man flying across the room and crashing into the wall with a roundhouse kick. Jace made it look easy. Bret attempted to keep his balance and actually came at Jace again.

This time Jace let go with a right uppercut to the head that once again sent the man flying from one side of the room to the other. When his body made contact with the opposite wall he slid to the floor like a sack of rotten potatoes.

The sight was unreal. Camera flashes filled the room. Jace's face was wrought with rage, his nostrils flaring, his mind and body not yet receiving the message it was over as he walked over to Bret, his fists clenched in anger. Jace was still in fight mode as two men stepped between him and his now unconscious—and no doubt soon to be former—manager. Their voices were low as they talked Jace down, assuring him it was over.

There was a moan and Bret struggled to sit up. Someone handed him a handkerchief and he held the cloth against his nose, not yet realizing that blood had soaked the front of his shirt.

Jace's eyes cut to Kelly. In that moment, he seemed to visibly calm down before a look of remorse and dismay flooded his features. He shrugged out of the men's hold and glanced at Bret, still lying on the floor, and then back at Kelly.

A moment passed between them before Jace turned and walked out of the room.

Fifteen

Jace entered his suite, letting the door close behind him. Shrugging out of his jacket, he tossed it onto a nearby chair, pulled off the tie and ripped open the dress shirt, sending the buttons flying. At the en suite bar he poured a triple and threw it down his throat. Bracing his arms against the countertop he stared at the image in the mirror. The contorted face that stared back, partially concealed by shadows, was not Jace Compton. It was a man with deadly eyes and a cold, menacing stare. The mouth was a thin straight line with deep grooves of leftover rage on either side. The white shirt hung open, bearing traces of Goldman's blood. Jace clenched his jaw as he stared at the face of George Compton in the mirror. His father had rematerialized and displayed all the trademark brutality and cruelty of Jace's childhood.

The beast had come out. Right in front of Kelly.

Jace poured another shot, downed it the same way and headed for the bathroom. Turning on the shower, he shucked the remaining clothes and stepped under the warm spray. He was still angry. He knew Bret was a pompous ass, knew he screwed around on his wife, knew his reputation in Hollywood circles was that of a ruthless, pushy, conniving, hard-nosed son of a bitch. But Jace had never witnessed him in full assault mode before tonight. It made it a thousand times worse that he'd set his sights on Kelly. She'd been so hesitant to attend the ball, and then to be accosted by a degenerate like Bret had Jace wishing he'd pounded the guy harder than he did.

But what churned in his gut was the knowledge that Kelly had witnessed everything. The shocked look on her face when he'd met her gaze before he turned and walked from the room would haunt him forever. Her eyes had been as wide as saucers, her hands clenched tightly in front of her as if in fright. She'd looked away from him to stare at the man lying on the floor, his face blotchy, his white dress shirt covered in blood. Jace couldn't be sure if it was shock or disbelief that froze her delicate features and made her skin lose some of its healthy color.

If there had ever been any hope he could keep Kelly in his life, hope that he wouldn't turn into his old man, he now knew with absolute certainty he could toss that dream into the trash. Someday it might be Kelly on the floor, her face bruised and bloodied. Just the thought made him physically sick.

Trudging out of the shower, he wrapped a towel around his waist, walked toward the en suite bar and poured himself another.

"Hi, baby." The sultry voice came from the general location of the bedroom. "We meet again so soon."

Jace froze. Flipping on the lights, he walked to the doorway of the bedroom and glared at the partially clothed woman in his bed, her long red hair covering her bare shoulders.

"Lena. *Goddammit.* What in the hell are you doing in here? Who let you in?" But Jace knew it wasn't the first time Lena had charmed her way into his private space, convincing an innocent employee it was her room. She and Bret, the two schemers, should get together. Or maybe they already had.

"Ah…come on, baby, don't be mad." The sound of her voice made him cold inside.

"This is not happening. You need to leave."

He grabbed her clothes from the chair and tossed them in

her direction. A contrived pout formed on her full lips as her brown eyes beseeched him to let her stay. Quite the actress.

"I can't believe you're going to throw me out. Why spend the night all by yourself?"

"Whether I do or don't is none of your goddamn business. What happened to Jack? Weren't you all into him?"

"Jack didn't work out." She sat up, not bothering to cover her bare chest. "I made a mistake, Jace. Can't you forgive one little mistake?"

"I don't care one way or the other, Lena." He settled his hands on his waist. "Whatever we had, if anything, ended a long time ago. I told you two years ago when you came up with that insane idea of pretending to be married, that was it for me. No more. Get dressed. Now. Then get out."

The pout still on her face, she grabbed her clothes and began to get dressed.

There was a persistent knocking at his door. *What now?* He glared at Lena. "If that's the press, Lena, so help me…"

She shook her head, her hands palms up. "No. At least it's nothing I had anything to do with." Standing, she pulled on her gown and began to fasten the buttons that ran the full length of the sparkling black evening dress and headed into the bathroom.

Jace took in a deep breath and clenched his hands into fists, wanting badly to reshape a wall.

Looking through the peephole in the door, he all but cringed. It wasn't reporters standing outside. It was Kelly. Running his hand over his face, he hesitated. He knew what she would think when she saw Lena. But after what she'd witnessed downstairs did it really make any difference? Swinging open the door, he stood back and she stepped inside the room.

"I just wanted to make sure you were okay."

"Yeah. I'm good." It was a sheer miracle he wasn't sitting in a jail cell. Again. "Kelly, there's something I need to tell you—"

"Jace, give me a call the next time you're—"

He heard Kelly's intake of breath as Lena walked back into the room, still buttoning her dress as she rounded the corner. The two women stared at each other.

"I'm…I'm sorry." Kelly bolted for the door. Luckily, Jace got there first.

"No. This is not what you think."

Lena smiled, her eyes sparkling in humorless amusement as she glided slowly toward the pair. "It never is." She leaned over casually and picked up her clutch, and then tossed her hair back over her shoulders in a practiced manner.

"This must be Kelly." She looked at Jace. "She is beautiful." She turned to Kelly. "Don't look so shocked, honey. Remember who you're with. This is Jace Compton's world. Better get used to it."

Firmly holding Kelly's wrist, he opened the door and Lena walked through it without a backward glance.

"Kelly, I did not invite her into this room. In fact, I'm not sure how the hell she got in."

"It's not really my business although you both being undressed was…convenient. Her timing is very good."

She glanced around the room, as though looking for a secret portal that would transport her magically far away from this place.

"Kelly?"

She tilted her head and her eyes found his. "I believe you, Jace. But Lena was right. I appreciate the glimpse into Hollywood's inner circles, but if it's all the same, I think I'd better stick with the small-town country bumpkins. Your ranch hands have better manners than most of the people here tonight." She shook her head as if in sad defeat. "There's so much more to life than…this." She attempted a small laugh that fell flat. "Is this usually the way your parties end? A few drinks, slugging it out, then a little bed-hopping with…whoever?"

Jace felt as if his heart had been hit by a meteorite. He'd

probably frightened her so badly that even coming to his room had taken every grain of intestinal fortitude she possessed. But what brought him to his knees was the knowledge almost everything she said was true.

"No, not always. Sometimes the police get involved and jail cells are added to the mix. I'm sorry you had to see what happened downstairs."

Jace didn't know what else to say. There was nothing he *could* say.

And only one thing would make this right with Kelly.

He had to end this. Now. Before he hurt her.

Bile rose in the back of his throat and his entire body tightened. He closed his eyes, dropped his head and grimaced in pure self-disgust.

What an idiot he'd been to even think of a future with Kelly. She wouldn't travel the globe with a newborn son. And she wasn't one to stay at home for months at a time waiting for him to return. And even if she was willing, he wouldn't ask that of her.

It would be an understatement to say she wouldn't be comfortable with the droves of media that would surround and follow her. Kelly would not sit back and ignore the ridiculous headlines claiming he'd had yet another affair. It would cause her to relive what her own father had done and the consequences they'd all suffered.

But all that aside, even if he walked away from films, all she would have was the beast inside him and no way of knowing what would set it off. Or when. The same monster she'd gotten only a small glimpse of tonight. It was a no-win scenario.

The very last thing she needed was mistreatment by an abusive man. God, he wanted to be part of her life, to make her, Henry and Matt part of his. He wanted Kelly until his mind and heart threatened to explode and sparks of desperation lit the darkness. But he knew, in this moment, it could never happen. He had no right to pursue her with his father's DNA running rampant through his veins.

"You were right. This is no life for you. It's no life for Henry."

He watched her. It was past time she knew the truth.

He caught her gaze and held it. His nostrils flared with the pain of what he was about to say. "What you saw tonight is who I am."

She stood in the doorway, the overhead lights making her an ethereal vision. He stepped back to the bar and poured another drink. It wouldn't be his last before the sun rose tomorrow.

"Jace? I don't understand."

"I'm trying to tell you I can't stop living this way because of who I am inside. I can't change it." He threw the amber liquid down his throat and turned to face her. "What I do for a living and all that goes with it provides an outlet. An escape from my own sick reality. It lets me drink myself into oblivion—" he held up the glass "—and the media just report a party. It lets me pound somebody—usually a professional but not always, like tonight—and release some of the rage. Makes for good headlines." He gave a false laugh at the ridiculousness of it. "Hell, they even pay me to do it. The travel, the new film locations, memorizing scripts, it keeps me from thinking. From remembering what I am inside. It helps prevent me from doing what you saw me do tonight. It's the only way I have to get through another day.

"I can't offer you the man you want, Kelly. I can't give you forever. I can't provide the home and the life you and Henry need. I can't be the husband you deserve. Ever." He clenched his jaw, determined to make her leave while she could. "I'm not even sure I can love you."

He watched her flinch as though she'd been shot. He stood helplessly as shock, then anguish, played across her fine features. Kelly bravely blinked back the tears that filled her eyes. He'd hurt her deeply, but she would be better off in the long run. Better off without him.

"After spending time with you, getting to really know you, any fool could see..." He clenched his jaw with a force that should have cracked teeth.

"See what, Jace?" Her voice was unsteady, barely a whisper. Her face had lost all of its color.

"That you don't belong here. You don't belong with me."

Kelly was a person who lived life from the heart. She was a woman who would fight to the death to protect her son, who got back on her feet every time life knocked her down, who made a home for her brother when there was no one else and kept his dreams of a future alive even at the cost of her own. A stubborn, tenacious woman who scorned pity and would rather chop off her nose than accept what she though was charity. A beautiful woman who needed to be loved and cherished—not abused. "You were right that first night, Kelly. The night we talked outside your house. I should have left then. I just didn't want to accept the inevitable."

Kelly nodded. She miraculously managed a smile without allowing even one tear to fall even though they filled her eyes, a tribute to her strength.

A brittle stillness filled the space around them, so rigid and taut with emotion the slightest movement would cause it to crack and bring the walls surrounding them tumbling down.

She turned to leave and paused when he said, "I wish things could have been different."

Without turning to face him she opened the door and walked out.

A rage filled Jace. A rage beyond anything he'd ever felt before and all directed inward, at himself. All hope turned to hopelessness. The monster had won. With a silent scream, he hurled the glass across the room into the mirror, shattering it into a million pieces. Like his heart.

* * *

A week later Jace sat in the meeting, wishing he were a thousand miles away. Anywhere would do. He absently twirled a pen in his fingers as producer Doug Hamrick went over the plans for filming his next big-budget blockbuster. Around the expansive conference table sat the director, assistant directors, five other actors, scriptwriters, technical advisers, and the attorneys and agents representing them all. Only Bret Goldman was noticeably absent. Jace had made sure of that, firing him before he'd ever left the ballroom.

Filming would last six to seven months with postproduction another four. The locations were some of the most exotic in the world. Hard as hell to reach, a challenge to film, but the ambiance couldn't be beat.

In front of Jace on the shiny mahogany table was the contract awarding him the leading role. It would afford him the opportunity for another best actor nomination along with the possibility of best picture of the year.

The mood in the room was jovial, the excitement and anticipation obvious in the faces of everyone who sat around the table. But as Jace idly listened to the questions and answers, his thoughts were of Kelly. Seven months was a long time to be away. It had never seemed so long before. But what in the hell else did he have to do? Kelly and his mom had flown back to Texas the day after the ball. He'd stayed over in LA for this meeting, hiding out at his house in Malibu, wondering how long Kelly would stay at the ranch.

The rolling surf that used to calm him couldn't touch the panic and utter devastation that festered inside. His mind scrambled to find a solution—*any* solution—that could keep Kelly in his life. But the same scenario bumped along, around and around, like a flat tire on a car going downhill, preventing him from catching a glimpse of hope.

He remembered the first time he ever saw Kelly, arguing with the guy in the feed store over the cost of a bag of oats. She'd won. No surprise there. Jace had carried the horse feed out to her truck, determined to find out her name and get a phone number before she disappeared. He remembered how her face radiated tenderness and natural beauty in the glow of the little candle on the table in the café later that evening.

Days later, when he'd taken her to the small motel, he'd immediately realized her inexperience. He'd been determined to show her what making love was really about, and that night would go down in the history books. She'd stripped him of every ounce of control he could find and made him wish for a lot more. She was so damn sexy yet so innocent in the ways of the world, so trusting of him, so eager to please. He was left speechless, shaken to his core and totally and completely enthralled.

And by the next morning, using a condom never entered his mind.

He'd asked her to dinner the following night. Partly to ensure she was okay and partly because she was so damned amazing he had to prove to himself she was for real. She accepted. And that night, after they'd eaten, he had taken her straight home to her grandfather's ranch even though it was the last thing he wanted to do.

Later that night, he'd been awakened by a light tapping on his guest cabin door. He'd opened it to find Kelly standing on the other side. Neither said a word. Both knew why she was there. The attraction worked both ways; one was not whole without the other. He pulled her into his arms and they didn't leave the hotel room for the next three days.

Later he'd secured the loan of two horses and together they roamed the hills and valleys of north Texas. They'd talked and laughed the day away, her naturally golden curls falling loose from the old brown hat she'd plopped on her head. They'd splashed in a pond surrounded by grass and cattails, fed each other olives they'd found tucked in one of the saddle bags, and made love under the shade of a willow tree on an old red blanket cushioned by thick native grasses. The memories were permanently etched in his mind.

It was in those moments when time hung suspended and his crazy world faded to nothing that he'd fallen in love with Kelly Michaels.

Kelly's charm went beyond physical beauty. It was the sparkle in her eyes when she laughed. It was in the way she held their son with such love and tenderness. It was the praise she heaped on her brother, always keeping alive the promise of a bright future. It was the soft, melodic sound of her voice and her inner strength and fortitude. It was the sparks that shot from her eyes when she was angry. Her intelligence and quick wit that kept Jace on his toes. She made him glad to be alive. No one else had ever done that.

His entire life had been built around the fear that he would become like his father. Despite his lifelong determination to remain detached, Kelly had found a way into his heart. She'd given him a child. A son. And he was still totally and completely in love with the mother of that child. But the reason they were not together—and never could be together—hadn't changed.

The vibration of his cell phone jerked him out of his reflections. Looking at the screen, he saw it was his mother. His mom knew he had this meeting. She wouldn't call unless it was important.

Jace excused himself from the conference room and stepped outside into the hall.

"Mom?"

"Jason." He could hear the quiet anguish in that one word. He had his answer. "Kelly's gone."

It was dark by the time Jace walked into the house. His mom was sitting at the kitchen bar, a cup of coffee in one hand, a well-used tissue in the other. Her eyes red-rimmed, her nose pink from crying.

"When did she leave?"

"Around three." His mother's voice was hoarse from the many tears she'd shed.

"Do you know where she went?"

"She went back to her house." Mona shook her head. "She promised she would stay in touch."

Jace could only nod. He'd pursued her. He'd taken advantage of her feelings for him and taken her to his bed all the while knowing he could give her no promises. Then he'd figuratively slapped her in the face, possibly broken her heart and stood three feet away, presenting the appearance of a cold unfeeling bastard, while she crumbled and bravely tried to hold on to her emotions, her self-respect. It was because of him and the son of a bitch who fathered him that she was gone now. He'd wanted her to walk away, to hate him if it helped her, and never look back.

He'd done his job well.

He walked to the bar, grabbed a bottle of whiskey, then proceeded to his office where he closed and locked the door. He'd drink a toast to the old man. Hell, why not?

He'd become just like him.

Sixteen

Jace entered the house, needing more coffee. His mother joined him in the kitchen. He knew she was worried. About him. About Kelly. About the situation. He looked like something dredged up from the pits of hell. Bloodshot eyes. Beard stubble. Maybe a little weight loss as well, but he didn't give a damn.

"Jason, talk to me."

He shrugged. "About what?"

"It's been over a month since Kelly left. Maybe it's time you talked to her."

"Let it go, Mom." He poured the fresh coffee into his mug.

She shook her head in frustration. "Jason—"

"Just drop it, okay? It's over. It's done. It's too late to go back. And I don't want to talk about it."

Jace had done what he'd had to do when he made Kelly leave. Out of respect he'd eventually have to give his mom some kind of explanation, but it wasn't going to happen today.

"Nothing is ever too late, Jason," she said softly. "Not as long as your heart is still beating."

With a polite nod, Jace stepped around her and headed back to the barn. The anguish of losing Kelly never let up. The pain had become a permanent extension of his body and mind. And always, with every breath, he questioned if he'd done the right thing. He'd finally stopped telling himself to let it go. He couldn't. He knew he never would.

The what-ifs plagued him. Night and day. What if his

love for her was enough to quiet the beast? In normal circumstances Kelly made happiness swell inside him. Even when those turquoise eyes shot bolts of fire in his direction because of something stupid he'd said, he felt the love for her that went to the marrow.

What if he'd done the wrong thing? What if they *could* have a life together? What if ten years from now it became apparent he'd thrown away something special for no good reason, something he would never find again? It was making him crazy.

Dammit to hell. During the day he barked at every hand on the ranch, throwing out threats that had them scrambling, the frustration and internal anger refusing to be contained. Two men had already quit. There would be more if he didn't get a handle on this. But he couldn't make himself give a damn. At night, he lay staring into the darkness. Only then did he let himself imagine going to her, holding her. Only then in the obscurity of a dream did he feel alive.

Shouts broke the silence. Glancing ahead, just outside the corral, his ranch hands circled two of their fellow cowboys who appeared determined to take each other out one punch at a time. Their faces were red, their anger obvious. These were not stuntmen rehearsing a future scene. These were men he employed, and he would not tolerate this kind of behavior.

Gritting his teeth, Jace hurried forward. The foreman stood steps away from the brawling men. "Somebody grab Decker. I'll get Colby."

Jace never slowed his stride. Before anyone moved forward per Sam's orders, Jace walked between the two men, grabbing one by the arm, slinging him to the ground. The other suffered a similar fate.

Jace continued to stand between them. "What in the hell is going on?" This was all he needed. The whole damn world was falling apart. "You have less than two seconds to explain or you're both out of here." His gaze shot from one to the other. The cowboys not involved in the fight stood quietly, waiting to see what Jace would do.

One of the men rubbed at the trickle of blood under his nose with the back of his hand. "He's been making passes at my wife."

Jace could hear the fury, the pain in the man's voice. "Is that true, Decker?"

Decker glared. "So what if I have? It wasn't like she gave me the cold shoulder."

"You son of a bitch," Colby growled and went for Decker again. Jace quickly halted his forward motion.

"That's it, Decker. Get your stuff and get off my property. Sam will tag along just to make sure you find your way." Jace turned his attention back to Colby, who still struggled to get free of Jace's hold. "Colby, let it go." He called to a couple of the cowboys. "Take him and stay with him until he cools off."

As the men hurried to follow his orders, Jace rubbed the back of his neck. Had everyone gone crazy? He had to sympathize. He knew exactly what Colby was feeling. Maybe his wife egged him on. Maybe she didn't. But Colby had a right to defend what was his. Normally a decent, hardworking man, he'd let his love for his wife blind him to everything but the need to protect her.

The breath died in Jace's throat. Is that what he'd been doing when he took out Bret? The epiphany almost blinded him. Why in the hell hadn't he seen it before? He hadn't lost himself in a mindless fit of rage. He'd done what he needed to do to stop Bret from hurting Kelly. To protect the woman he loved. There was a difference. A big difference.

Stunned from the belated realization, Jace was equally elated and afraid.

Had the realization come too late?

The television blared with the intended purpose of ensuring Kelly didn't have a chance to think. It wasn't working.

Regardless of what she did to try to keep her mind from dwelling on Jace, nothing worked. She grabbed the remote and switched it off.

Returning to the kitchen, she turned on the oven and finished stirring the homemade dressing. It was her offering to Gerri's family for her mother's birthday.

The last thing Kelly wanted was to be around people but Gerri insisted she was part of the family and refused to take no for an answer. Kelly had finally given in to her friend since second grade. It seemed the least she could do to repay Gerri for her many kindnesses and concern since Kelly left the ranch.

Gerri had asked if she could take the baby, reminding her how much her mother wanted to see him. When Gerri's brother stopped to pick her up, Kelly agreed, saying she would finish the dressing and follow in Gerri's car. At least that was the plan.

She spooned the mix into the baking pan, shoved it into the oven and set the timer. After washing the bowl and utensils, she ventured into the small living room and plopped down on a chair. Tomorrow she would call Mona. She wanted to hear her voice. She needed to hear Jace's voice, too, and feel his arms around her, but that was not going to happen. Ever.

Picking up a magazine, she idly paged through it. If she dwelled one more second on Jace she would go crazy. She didn't want to go to Gerri's mother's birthday party with her eyes red and puffy. Since that night at the hotel in LA, she couldn't seem to stop crying. Trying to make sense out of what had happened left her even more confused. The pain never ended.

The timer on the oven began to ding. She pushed herself out of the chair and walked to the kitchen and removed the dressing from the oven before turning it off. What had made Jace go from a person who had worked to rebuild her trust and made her think he loved her to suddenly assur-

ing her she didn't belong in his life? Apparently she was
good enough while they were isolated at the ranch but not
good enough to fit into his life in Hollywood. She'd known
she didn't belong, but he'd insisted she was wrong. Why?
Why had he even bothered? She had so many questions that
would never be answered.

A knock on the apartment door broke into her thoughts.
Frowning, she walked back to the living room. She opened
the door and the shock that hit her was like the blow of a
baseball bat to the solar plexus.

Jace stood on the doorstep. He wasn't smiling. His green
eyes carried a haunted look, as though he wasn't sure he
should be here. But his clenched jaw established his determination; he wasn't going anywhere. "Can we talk?"

Her mind tried to grasp the realization he was here. "I
think you've already said everything there is to say."

"No, I haven't. Will you invite me in? Or are we going
to argue out on the sidewalk?"

"*I'm* not going to argue at all."

"That might be a first." His attempt at humor fell flat.
He forced a smile that didn't reach his eyes.

Glaring, she turned away but left the door open. If he
wanted to come in she wouldn't try to stop him, but she
wasn't going to invite him. Her heart pounded so hard it
was difficult to breathe.

Why is he here?

Kelly moved to the center of the room, wrapping her
arms tightly around herself in an effort to control the storm
of emotions raging through her. She wanted him to go. She
wanted to put her arms around him and never let him go.
His presence caused the blood to race through her veins
while her mouth went dry and tears stung the back of her
eyes. She'd been an emotional wreck for weeks. She couldn't
sleep. She didn't want food. She only wanted to scream and
pound on his chest and demand that he explain *why*. Now

was her chance and she couldn't look at him. She was down two strikes and already out. She couldn't survive a third.

Jace stood in front of her as though waiting for something. Finally she glanced at him. He held her gaze and didn't let go. He bore the same haunted look she saw when she looked in the mirror.

"I just have one question."

"Really? I have about a hundred."

"Do you love me, Kelly?"

"What?" By her reaction, he clearly knew she thought he was crazy.

"If I had a regular job, say…as a ranch hand. Would you give me a second chance?"

She struggled to hold back the tears. She loved him with all of her heart. But what was the point of these questions? "You're not a ranch hand. I think we've sufficiently cleared up that little misunderstanding."

He stepped up to her. "Are you in love with me?" He repeated the question, his voice a rough demand. "After what I did…is it even possible?"

It was hard to answer a pointless question.

"Kelly?"

"What's the reason for this, Jace? Did you come all this way, go to all this trouble just to catch me off guard and knock me down again?" She was furious. She hated him. She loved him. "I don't get it. I really don't. Is this what you do? You just play with people? Play with their emotions?"

"I guess I'll take that as a no."

"What in the hell do you expect me to say? You…you made it clear you couldn't love me. You said I didn't belong in your life. I'm not good enough and I never will be. At least for once you were honest."

"That's not what I meant," he bellowed. He was getting angry. *Well, bring it on, babycakes.* He had a long way to go to equal what she was feeling.

"Then a month later you show up here, asking if I love

you? You're a jackass, Compton. Worse, you're…you're…
deranged."

"I guess that really is a no." He nodded his acceptance
and turned to leave.

"Most of the attendees at Mona's ball would say the answer to your question is a resounding no. I don't love you.
Apparently, I got my hooks in deep enough to haul in some
big bucks without letting my heart get involved."

He spun around and gripped her shoulders. "Kelly, do
you love me?"

She could sense he wanted to shake her, but he merely
held her instead.

"Are you in love with me?" This time his voice was soft,
almost a plea.

"Yes." It was only a whisper, the best she could do, but
he heard her. "Are you happy now? What…did this win
some kind of bet? Do I get an award for the biggest fool
of the year?"

At her confession, he closed his eyes and seemed to relax.
"Thank God."

"Why?"

"Because I'm in love with you."

"Oh, please."

"You're the only woman I've ever said that to. I've never
been in love before, Kelly."

"Jace…" She shook her head. "You're not in love now. I
appreciate the sentiments, I guess. But this is not love. Let
me clue you in. Treating someone like you treated me in
LA is not love. Not even close."

He took a deep breath and blew it out, his hand wiping
the lower portion of his face.

"I said some really stupid things, but for a good reason.
I was trying to protect you that night at the hotel."

"Do I honestly have to tell you how ridiculous you sound?"

"My own father was bad news, Kelly. He was in and out
of prison most of my life. And he was a mean son of a bitch.

He beat Mom. She left him so many times, she had him arrested, tried to find a place we could hide. But he found us. And it was bad. She fought back, but he was so much bigger than she was. When I tried to stop it, he turned on me. I was twelve when he broke my jaw. Thirteen when he busted six ribs. He didn't give a damn. He just wanted those around him to hurt as much as he did. To pay for his mistakes. He screwed up his life and he wasn't man enough to admit it."

Jace let out a breath. "I've lived with the very real possibility that someday I'll become just like him. It's in my genes. I didn't want you or Henry anywhere around when that day came. I was afraid if you loved me, if I didn't make you leave, you'd stay."

She frowned. He was serious. "You will never be like that, Jace."

"In the past month, I finally realized it came down to a choice. Beg you to stay in my life and run the risk I might someday become…abusive. Or go on with my life as it has been—empty, lonely, wanting the things most men take for granted. I'm a selfish bastard, Kelly. I need you. I can't live the rest of my life knowing I gave up the best thing that ever came into it. And if you'll give me a chance, I'll fight with every breath I take each and every day to keep the monster at bay. I will not hurt you, Kelly. Ever."

His eyes beseeched her. "Come back to the ranch with me. Marry me. Marry me for no reason other than I want you to be my wife. Because I love you."

Kelly didn't know how to take all this in. Was he telling her the truth? Did he actually believe he would hurt her?

"I've quit acting, Kelly," he said. "I never signed the contract for the new film. I walked out. It took me a while to get it through my thick head and understand what you were saying. You and Henry are so much more important than making films."

She looked up into his eyes and the tears brimmed in hers. She clamped her hand over her mouth. *What had she done?* "Jace, no. No. I didn't have the right to demand you change your life if you wanted to be part of Henry's. Oh God. That was wrong. You're leaving your career, what you love, for the wrong reason. Eventually you'll hate me for it. Don't you see? Don't do it, Jace. You can see your son whenever you want. Please don't pity me and think giving up your career will make anything right."

A look of dark humor settled into his handsome features. "*Pity?* You are the most stubborn, hardheaded female I have ever run across in my life. Where in the hell do you get these crazy ideas? I don't pity you, Kelly. I respect the hell out of you. What…you think I would pity you for making a home for Matt and Henry by working your ass off when you had no one else? You think I pity you for coming to the ranch even though you hated me, because it was a safer place for Henry? Take pity out of your vocabulary because there is no pity. Not for you. But there is respect. A lot of respect.

"I gave up the film career because I'm tired of it." Jace watched her closely, as though she might bolt and run. "I'm tired of the travel, the media circus, keeping up appearances, the lies…all of it. You were right when you said there was so much more to life. If I had any doubts I needed to get out, those were wiped clean the night of Mom's charity event. I saw everything, the people, the bullshit, all of it through your eyes. When Bret attacked you… When you walked into my room and saw Lena. I never want to relive any of that again."

"I knew you were telling the truth about Lena. I told you I believed you. As far as that creep, that wasn't cruelty, Jace. It wasn't a monster inside you. You were protecting me." She reached out to him. "I've never had anyone… No one has ever done that for me."

"Kelly, I want a home and a family." He pulled her closer. "I want to raise horses. And all of it has to include you. It's the reason I bought that ranch."

"What?"

"I could have purchased land anywhere. But you were here." Jace reached out and touched her face. "Be my wife, Kelly. Be the mother of my children. You showed me how good life could be. Don't take that dream away. Please give us another chance."

He was an award-winning actor. But she knew he spoke from his heart. She closed her eyes, the reality almost too much to take in. The only man she'd ever loved was offering her more than she'd ever dared to dream.

"If you love me, we can make this work. I haven't been with another woman since Henry was conceived. I just... there was no one... I don't *want* anyone else, Kelly, and I've had a year to think about that. I can't change what your father did, but I'm not him. I can never undo all you've been through because of me. All I can do is promise, if you'll have me, I'll spend the rest of my life making the rest of your life as good as I possibly can."

His hand went under her chin, gently raising her lips to his. In that moment, she gave him her heart, her trust, her love, returning his kiss with everything she had.

"I love you, Jace." She fell into his arms and the tears of joy fell down her face. He kissed her deeply, passionately, letting his hunger for her free, holding her tightly as though he would never let her go, as though he couldn't get close enough. And Kelly kissed him back with every ounce of love she had for this incredible, amazing, complex man. Her hands slipped up his chest.

"You're still a moron," she whispered against his lips.

"What?"

"What in the hell took you so long?"

He laughed. "Woman, you make me crazy." Then all humor left his voice and was replaced with earnest desperation. "Marry me. Now. Today. As soon as we can arrange it. Say yes. I need to wake up next to you every morning. Make love to you every night. I want a family. I want kids. I hope you do."

She chewed her lower lip as she enthusiastically nodded in agreement. He cupped her face in his hands. "There is nothing I want more than to make you pregnant again." His deep voice made her shiver. "But this time I want to look into those amazing blue eyes when we conceive our next child. I want to know the instant it happens. I want to know you see the love in my face. But you're going to have a ring on your finger when I do."

"Jace... Yes. I love y—"

Jace's mouth covered hers, with a passion she hoped would last forever. No longer would she have to gaze up at the night sky. She had found her star, and in his arms was exactly where she needed to be.

* * * * *

*If you loved this book from
Lauren Canan,
pick up her debut novel*

TERMS OF A TEXAS MARRIAGE.

Available now from Harlequin Desire!

*If you're on Twitter, tell us what you think of
Harlequin Desire! #harlequindesire*

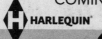

REQUEST YOUR FREE BOOKS!
2 FREE NOVELS PLUS 2 FREE GIFTS!

H HARLEQUIN®

Desire

ALWAYS POWERFUL, PASSIONATE AND PROVOCATIVE

YES! Please send me 2 FREE Harlequin® Desire novels and my 2 FREE gifts (gifts are worth about $10). After receiving them, if I don't wish to receive any more books, I can return the shipping statement marked "cancel." If I don't cancel, I will receive 6 brand-new novels every month and be billed just $4.55 per book in the U.S. or $5.24 per book in Canada. That's a savings of at least 13% off the cover price! It's quite a bargain! Shipping and handling is just 50¢ per book in the U.S. and 75¢ per book in Canada.* I understand that accepting the 2 free books and gifts places me under no obligation to buy anything. I can always return a shipment and cancel at any time. Even if I never buy another book, the two free books and gifts are mine to keep forever.

225/326 HDN GH2P

Name	(PLEASE PRINT)	
Address		Apt. #
City	State/Prov.	Zip/Postal Code

Signature (if under 18, a parent or guardian must sign)

Mail to the **Reader Service:**

IN U.S.A.: P.O. Box 1867, Buffalo, NY 14240-1867
IN CANADA: P.O. Box 609, Fort Erie, Ontario L2A 5X3

Want to try two free books from another line?
Call 1-800-873-8635 or visit www.ReaderService.com.

* Terms and prices subject to change without notice. Prices do not include applicable taxes. Sales tax applicable in N.Y. Canadian residents will be charged applicable taxes. Offer not valid in Quebec. This offer is limited to one order per household. Not valid for current subscribers to Harlequin Desire books. All orders subject to credit approval. Credit or debit balances in a customer's account(s) may be offset by any other outstanding balance owed by or to the customer. Please allow 4 to 6 weeks for delivery. Offer available while quantities last.

Your Privacy—The Reader Service is committed to protecting your privacy. Our Privacy Policy is available online at www.ReaderService.com or upon request from the Reader Service.

We make a portion of our mailing list available to reputable third parties that offer products we believe may interest you. If you prefer that we not exchange your name with third parties, or if you wish to clarify or modify your communication preferences, please visit us at www.ReaderService.com/consumerchoice or write to us at Reader Service Preference Service, P.O. Box 9062, Buffalo, NY 14240-9062. Include your complete name and address.

HDI5

The door opened and there she was. He'd been prepared
for a spinsterish female, a librarian type.

This woman was a surprise.

She wore black pants and a crimson blouse with a
short black jacket over it. Her thick dark red hair fell
in heavy waves around her shoulders. She was tall and
curvy enough to make a man's mouth water. Her green
eyes, not hidden behind the glasses she'd worn in her
photo, were artfully enhanced and shone like sunlight in a
forest. And the steady, even stare she sent Brady told him
that she also had strength. Nothing hotter than a gorgeous
woman with a strong sense of self. Unexpectedly, he felt
a punch of desire that hit him harder than anything he'd
ever experienced before.

"Brady Finn?"

"That's right. Ms. Donovan?" He stood up and
waited as she crossed the room to him, her right hand
outstretched. She moved with a slow, easy grace that
made him think of silk sheets, moonlit nights and the soft
slide of skin against skin. Damn.

"It's Aine, please."

"How was your flight?" He wanted to steer the conversation into the banal so his mind would have nothing else to torment him with.

"Lovely, thanks," she said shortly and lifted her chin a notch. "Is that what we're to talk about, then? My flight? My hotel? I wonder that you care what I think. Perhaps we could speak, instead, about the fact that twice now you've not showed the slightest interest in keeping your appointments with me."

Brady sat back, surprised at her nerve. Not many employees would risk making their new boss angry. "Twice?"

"You sent a car for me at the airport and again at the hotel. I wonder why a man who takes the trouble to fly his hotel manager halfway around the world can't be bothered to cross the street to meet her in person."

When Brady had seen her photo, he'd thought *efficient*, *cool*, *dispassionate*. Now he had to revise those thoughts entirely. There was fire here, sparking in her eyes and practically humming in the air around her.

Damned if he didn't like it.

It was more than simple desire he felt now—there was respect, as well. Which meant he was in more trouble here than he would have thought.

Need to find out just how this business venture goes?
Don't miss HAVING HER BOSS'S BABY
by USA TODAY *bestselling author Maureen Child*

Available August 2015

www.Harlequin.com

Love the Harlequin book
you just read?

Your opinion matters.

Review this book on your favorite
book site, review site, blog or your own
social media properties and share
your opinion with other readers!

JUST CAN'T GET ENOUGH?

Join our social communities
and talk to us online.

You will have access to the latest
news on upcoming titles and special
promotions, but most importantly,
you can talk to other fans about your
favorite Harlequin reads.

Harlequin.com/Community

Facebook.com/HarlequinBooks

Twitter.com/HarlequinBooks

Pinterest.com/HarlequinBooks

THE WORLD IS BETTER WITH

Romance

Harlequin has everything from contemporary, passionate and heartwarming to suspenseful and inspirational stories.

Whatever your mood, we have a romance just for you!